THE HORSE RACE
HANDICAPPER'S DREAM

Jim Schwartz

DonHanna Press
Los Angeles CA 2014

Author photo and book design: Baz Here

Cover art: Linda Bladen

ISBN: 978-1500893316

DonHanna Press
245 S Serrano Ave
Suite 313
Los Angeles, California 90004 USA

Printed in the United States of America

To Donna, Hanna, Ollie, John,
my parents, and the thoroughbred

"When one is handicapping on the highest level one is not predicting the future, one is creating it. Let me repeat: when one is handicapping at the highest level one is not predicting the future, one is creating it. The way you handicap the race is the only way it can come out."

– Charles Lackey, World Series Of Handicapping Champion

CHAPTER ONE

At first glance, it was hard to tell if the racetrack was open or closed. The outer grandstand was almost completely deserted. Wisps of paper, mostly losing tickets, skidded across the black tarmac that abutted the track. The only sign of life was the tote board, blinking with the odds for the eighth and final race.

It was ten minutes before post time on this dreary late spring day at Hollywood Park in Inglewood, California. It was unseasonably cold, in the fifties and it had been raining intermittently throughout the day. Only hardy souls ventured to the track on a day like this. Those lucky enough to have a few bucks in their pockets after surviving seven races were huddled inside around TV monitors, drinking coffee or something more fortifying. Most hadn't watched a live race in years.

With seven minutes to post the bedraggled band of $20,000 maidens was led onto the track. If one was trying to find a bounce in the step of any of them, one would have been unsuccessful. These were bottom of the barrel horses still trying to win their first race. It was hard to believe one of these nags could physically win a race.

The jockeys who sat astride these steeds were also, for the most part, running on tough times. Few successful jockeys would stick around for a cheap race on a dreary Thursday at Hollywood Park. Several of the riders in the race sported poor winning percentages, riders hungry for a victory. Others were grizzled veterans hoping for one last trip to the winners circle. There were a couple of untested apprentices, riders learning the ropes. Only John Rubin, the talented, young rider of the eight horse, Princess Bride, had been competing with any success. That explained why his horse was the 5-2 favorite. Certainly there was nothing in the way the horse had run in its four previous races to warrant the support.

A few minutes before the horses were to be loaded into the gate dense fog rolled in. It was driven by a jet stream zipping down the coast from the north and soon shrouded the track in a sea of billowy grey. With one minute to post, the stewards were so concerned about the lack of visibility they thought about canceling the race. But they were afraid to antagonize the patrons and horsemen. They decided to let the jockeys make the call, knowing these particular jockeys would have ridden in a monsoon as they had little to prove and nothing to lose... except Rubin. He was the kind of jockey who was gaining a reputation as a tough competitor. He wasn't the type to step away from a challenge.

Finally the motley band was loaded into the gate. The eight steeds were to travel six furlongs or three quarters of a mile. It took a while to load the eight into their stalls. Several were bad actors who had to be forcibly pushed into the gate. One reared at the sight of a seagull taking off. Eventually they were all in. Princess Bride, the 9-5 favorite, loaded into the last stall.

The track announcer, Vince Long, peered through his high-powered Canon Ultra-Optics at the gate. "They're all in, I think," he intoned. Long was regarded as one of the most accurate race callers in the country. "It is now post time. Starter Richards is waiting to open the gates. There's a little milling about by the four horse Chester but...they're off! Along the inside, Jewel's Crown rushes up, Buffy is second, on the outside Princess Bride is there and... and...gosh, I can't see 'em!" The horses disappeared into a fogbank. All Long saw was a wall of grey.

"They're moving down the backstretch, I assume. At about this point, they should be at the quarter pole and...wait...there they are...they're going around the far turn and Chester has the lead by about two lengths, Jewel's Crown hugs the inside second, Rhythm Dancer in the orange silks moves into third and the rest…are a long way back and…I lost them, folks…and…and…here they are again! Chester has now opened up by about six lengths, Rhythm Dancer is moving into second, Jewel's Crown is back to third…Marvin the Martian chugs into fourth, Betty Boop in fifth and the rest, well, we'll catch up with them when they come out of the fog. In the meantime Chester is the easiest kind of winner, Rhythm Dancer will complete the exacta, Marvin The Martian the trifecta. Then it's Betty Boop, a tiring Jewel's Crown, Lex's Candlelight, Werbly… and there's not a trace of Princess Bride! Princess Bride has apparently not finished the race. Let's hope for the sake of the horse and rider Rubin they're alright."

The two track ambulances were already carefully threading their way through the fog, going five miles an hour instead of the usual fifty. Visibility was less than three feet. They listened for cries, whinnying, moans, anything that might lead them to the horse and rider. They feared the worst. The drivers and vets in the ambulances knew how dangerous it was to ride in such conditions.

The ambulances circled the track fifteen times. They covered every inch of the artificial surface, every square centimeter. By the time the police called off their final search seven hours later, just after midnight, everybody was pretty much convinced that the impossible had happened.

Princess Bride and promising jockey Rubin had vanished into thin air.

CHAPTER TWO

I was traveling in a car with several scraggly members of a blues band. One of the band members strummed a guitar, another banged a bongo.

We got to a stage. I wanted to listen to the band but I saw some guys playing the horses. I was walking into the racetrack when a plane came in, flying low. I ran, saw a subway tunnel and ducked down the steps. I jumped onto a train. I heard an explosion. Through the back door of the subway car I saw the world implode into smoke and ash. A fireball raced down the tracks. As it was about to engulf us we sped out of a tunnel.

I jumped off the train. A pretty girl approached. As she went to kiss me I saw my brother, still dressed in the cerise jockey silks he was wearing the day he disappeared. He waved. The girl pulled me towards her. As I went to embrace her I felt the earth jolt violently.

"Honey," I heard a voice call. "Honey."

As I struggled to make out the voice I saw my wife of two years, Debra, dressed in her cute purple pajamas, leaning over and shaking me.

"You were moaning again," she was saying. "Another nightmare?"

"The same one," I slurred.

"Dreams'll do that."

"He was waving to me. He wanted me to go to him." I left out the part about the girl.

"Was it the same, with the bomb and all?"

"Yeah," I said. "What time is it?"

"A little after six."

"I might as well get up".

"Wait a second," Debra said. "You have a cute little ribbon of dried saliva on your chin. Let me lick it off."

"No," I said, gently pushing her away and getting out of bed.

"Some fun you are."

It was my custom to work on my screenplay upon awakening, knowing that my most creative thoughts, such as they were, lay closest to the subconscious rumblings of my sleep-soul. When I reached the bathroom I realized I had an erection. It was lucky Debra hadn't noticed. I leaned forward and braced myself against the wall with one hand in an effort to guide the thin stream into the toilet. When I got back to the bed Debra had a cup of coffee for me. We sat in bed sipping, not saying much.

When I finished my coffee, I kissed her on the cheek, put on a robe, and shuffled into the portion of our small living room we had partitioned with a flimsy Japanese folding wall. It was my writing nook.

I picked up a pen and stared at the legal pad. I had been outlining my screenplay about a nerdy young Jewish man who idolizes the Mafia. He yearns to be a hero. Through a series of odd occurrences he meets an aging mobster who mentors him. The story is about the young man coming to grips with his cowardice.

I stared at the page for the longest time. Writing was impossible, because the page was filled with my jockey brother John's face, staring at me, and he was mouthing the words: "Help me, Sid. Help me."

CHAPTER THREE

I came into the kitchen to find Debra eating a healthy bowl of something crunchy and grainy and completely unappealing.

"Hi sweetie," she said. "Back so soon?"

I went to the cupboard and got a huge box of Sugar Smacks. We bought it at Costco so it weighed about forty pounds. I poured some into a bowl, covered it with whole milk, and sat across from her at our small Formica kitchen table.

"You know, that's a salad bowl," she said.

"Looks like a bowl to me."

"Sid, that's the salad bowl, the bowl you put ALL the salad in and serve from." I looked down. It still looked normal.

"Sugar, sugar, sugar," she said.

"Your powers of observation are at an all time high, Deb," I said filling my face with a big spoonful.

"I'll refuse to inject your insulin," she said.

"Whatever".

She shrugged and finished her rabbit food. I ate with a steady determination, reading the almost non-existent sports section of the New York Times.

"Look at this," Deb said, glancing at the New York Post. Being news-obsessed, we were a two paper family. "There's a report of aliens landing on the West Side Highway last night."

"No shit. What were they driving?"

"Really. Somebody saw lights and a huge saucer like thing."

"Doesn't that sort of thing usually happen in Iowa?"

"Yeah, but these are strange times."

Strange times indeed. As I chomped away I thought about my younger brother John, the star of our family, a little shrimp who instead of letting his 4'2" height be a detriment was on his way to becoming a great jockey. We were so proud. The great irony was he made it in a sport, horse racing, that almost destroyed me.

Maybe that's why he became a jockey Because he wanted to avenge my defeat. Maybe that wasn't it at all. But it was a nice theory and in his absence it was mine. I finished the bowl of cereal, lifted it to my mouth and drank the half- inch of remaining sweetened milk. I sat back and felt a fart push toward my sphincter. Deb and I had been together for more than eight years and I had yet to fart in front of her. I toyed with the idea of getting another bowl of cereal.

"Don't even think about it," Deb said. "You just set a land speed record." She came up behind me and opened her robe. She was about 5'3" and thin. She rubbed her small tits on the back of my neck. I felt her nipples harden. I reached back and kneaded her right breast. I heard her moan, or maybe it was me. She had long nipples and she liked them pinched and sucked hard. She leaned over and put her tongue in my ear, kissed my neck. I turned and our lips met. She pulled back, touched her lips gently to mine, let her tongue skim provocatively. I needed her, wanted my tongue in her mouth and my cock in her pussy. I needed her moistness to envelope me. I carried her to the bedroom.

I locked the door behind us.

CHAPTER FOUR

Debra and I got along because we loved each other and required very little of one another. She had her private-duty nursing and painting. I had my AA and GA meetings, writing, and part time cabbie job.

We sought refuge in sex, conversation, the simple act of watching imbecilic TV shows, and eating. I'm not sure why we married, although I would say our decision almost killed a couple of sets of parents.

Deb's parents tried to talk her out of it. When I met Deb I was living in a flophouse, surviving on beer and cheese sandwiches. She more or less saved my life. Her parents weren't enthusiastic about her hitching her wagon to a newly sober thirty-six year old whose career high point was getting nosed out of a huge Pick Six at the Meadowlands and then attempting to walk back from the track to Manhattan by the most direct route, through the Secaucus swamplands. As for my parents, I could have married the woman judged most perfect by God and authenticated as such with a deific stamp on her ass and they still wouldn't have liked her. Maybe there was an act of defiance in our getting married. Whatever the reason, it felt good.

It was two days after our second wedding anniversary when my jockey brother John disappeared. We had just returned from John's Pizzeria on Bleecker Street. We settled in to watch the 11pm headlines on Channel 7, the worst news station in the world. We found it fun guessing if the stories were true or not. It was like a game show.

It was the lead story. If it wasn't my brother, I would have laughed at the absurdity. As it was, it was with true horror that I watched Carol Sussman, the pert and fuckable anchor, work her collagen-glossed lips into a pout and say, "In a story that has to rank among the most bizarre in the annals of sports, a jockey and his horse disappeared during the running of a race in Southern California today." I spent the rest of the sound bite squeezing Deb's hand so hard that she had to run it under ice water during the commercials. Seconds after the story ended, my parents were on the line. The incredulity is still there, three months after the "incident."

Initially we all thought there was a logical explanation and John would turn up, the engineer of a practical joke. As the days dragged on into weeks and the best investigative minds in the world remained baffled, our hopes turned to despair and for the most of the family, acceptance. I was headed that way too, until my nightly dreams of Armageddon starring my brother. He refused to let me believe he was gone. My inability to help him made me more aware of my failure as a human being than any alcoholic defeat.

Because of the dreams I was the only one who kept out hope that John was alive. I believed he was in a limbo I might access. Debra noticed a difference in me. She said my new brooding self was interesting, a welcome change from the AA missionary who went on laughing and forgiving and yammering about the glory of God's Will.

Maybe if Debra wasn't so accepting of my depression I would have done something about it. Instead I craved more of it, as a boozehound craved that second drink.

I obsessed on how I could find and save my brother. My need was fueled by postcards which came to my apartment addressed to "Resident", postmarked Los Angeles. On the front of the postcard was a picture of a motel. It was a simple sandstone building with purple neon lettering on a large signs in front saying SURF MOTEL - FREE HBO and AIR-CONDITIONING. Several palm trees and a blue ocean were just beneath the lettering. It looked like my kind of place.

CHAPTER FIVE

"Hi," I said, "my name Is Sid and I'm a compulsive gambler." The eight dour, middle-aged men clapped like I was the local talent at the Holiday Inn on a weeknight. "I guess I'm supposed to share for a couple of minutes so here goes. First of all, I'm not really a compulsive gambler in the true sense. I mean I am but it's only when I have a few drinks in me that I'm off to the races, so to speak."

A couple of snickers.

"It began in high school. Schoolwork came easy. I was pretty bored by everything except women and I wasn't very lucky in that department. Some friends took me to Aqueduct racetrack. It was like I had died and gone to heaven. I made it my life's mission to win at the track. I read every book on horse race handicapping and when I graduated with a degree in psychology I went to the track every available minute. What I didn't realize was that the difference between theory and winning was the difference between knowing what the coach expected in practice and executing on game day. My first few years of playing were marked by occasional wins but mostly bad losses. Although I chased I wasn't really a compulsive gambler. When the fear of losing set in I crossed the line. Every losing bet increased the fear. I couldn't sleep, couldn't eat. I worked at various jobs selling stuff. I did well in the cable TV and garment industries but found nine to five jobs didn't suit my racetrack needs.

I started driving a cab two or three nights a week. The rest of the time I read my racetrack books, kept detailed notes on the horses, and went to the track. Although my knowledge increased the fear persisted. I found having a few beers before and during the races reduced the fear. This was a relief, but now I was trying to perform subtle intellectual and intuitive tasks while looped. For years I drank and played the horses. There were times when I felt I knew more than any handicapper alive. Handicapping was the only thing that was important to me. I stopped caring about anything else. I lived in a small, dirty apartment. I studied the Racing Form. I slept with it on my pillow. I stopped watching TV and I rarely thought about women. I would drive the cab, drink beer, and go to the track. Every once in a while the loneliness peeked though. It occurred to me that I might have a problem. I tried to stop handicapping but could not. Only the Racing Form gave me joy. One night I was in bed and I started crying. It was a sadness I had never experienced. A few beers cheered me up but only for a while. I started seeing a shrink. She told me I had to keep things in perspective, that my handicapping and drinking was taking over my soul and if I wasn't careful I might not be able to return. I was frightened but I couldn't stop handicapping. I started to win. I hit some big payoffs. It was weird. Even when I won I had this sense of loss.

At that time I had a dog. I really loved that guy. One night when I came home the dog was real sick and I knew I had to take him to the vet. I decided to do it first thing in the morning. But that day there were a couple horses I liked. I went to Aqueduct. When I got home my dog was dead.

Within a week I was drinking a 12-pack by noon. Within a month I had moved out of my apartment and was living in a flophouse, driving drunk and playing the ponies. I would have died except for an angel who came into my life. We met in my taxicab. We talked. It had been so long since I shared myself with a woman. The feeling of emptiness disappeared. I got sober and abstinent, at first for her, then for God, then for myself.

We have a good life together. We have been married for over two years. There are times when I think of all the knowledge I have and all the time I spent mastering handicapping. I let go of those thoughts as I know the cost. I let go and let God, knowing that I can't do it myself. Thanks for letting me share."

CHAPTER SIX

As part of my GA program I never looked at the horse entries, watched race replays on TV, read articles about racing, or placed myself in situations where betting took place, unless I had business there. Which meant unless one of my fares was going to Atlantic City or the track, real long shots, I wasn't around the action. If the seed of gambling wasn't planted it couldn't grow into a carnivorous bush and consume me.

My brother's disappearance threw a crimp into the works. Since he was a jockey, every time I thought of him I thought of the races. It was like recollecting a great love, someone whose touch, smell, and embrace you miss. I continually pondered the disappearance.

Years before, under equally foggy conditions at a little track in Louisiana, a jockey hid his horse in a fogbank while the rest of the field negotiated the mile and one eighth race. He rejoined them as they made their way around the final turn. With a quick burst of speed the fresh horse roared by the tired competition and won easily. If the jockey used better judgment and didn't win the race by twenty-nine lengths, no one would have been the wiser. As it was, an investigation ensued, the truth came out and the jockey was suspended for ten years. The horse was held blameless.

This incident was hardly of the magnitude of what happened

to my brother. But it involved fog and subterfuge. I thought of races I had watched in fog, rain, snow, sleet, hail and gusts of wind so severe it appeared the horses were running sideways. I thought of wins and losses under any and all climatic conditions. I thought of how the elements can influence the outcome of races.

Rain at one track increases the chances of the speed horses; at another, the closers. Rain at some tracks gives the edge to horses on the inside, at others the outside. It depends on the composition of the topsoil and whether the surface is sealed prior to the rain or harrowed to full depth prior to the precipitation. At Hollywood Park, where my brother disappeared, the track was composed of a synthetic surface called Cushion Track. It theoretically should have held up to the elements. But who knew for sure? My mind worked out scenarios endlessly, starting with my brother and ending up somewhere else completely. I had to fight to stay earthbound.

It was my custom to share my writing with Debra in the evening before the 11 o'clock news. Inevitably she was supportive. She said I was the greatest writer since Dr. Seuss. I wondered about the compliment.

Of my six finished screenplays only one got action. It was about a demonic school principal whose plan was to turn the boys into a military juggernaut and take the city hostage. It was non-autobiographical. A Hasidic Rabbi, of all people, paid me $3,000 for a two- year option. I wasn't sure if the story would work set in a Yeshiva but, hey, cash was cash. Because of my increasing inability to concentrate, work on the screenplay went poorly.

"You seem to be losing focus," Debra said. "I can't tell whose story it is."

"You read ten pages tonight. What can be resolved in ten pages?"

"You're eighty pages in. I should know whose story it is."

Ah, I thought. This is how it works. They turn against you, with a glance, then words, mere words, then with the pent up bile of actions.

But of course, she was right. I had no idea what I was doing in the screenplay or in my life. I was losing my way and I was uncertain how to get back on the path. Most troubling, there seemed to be nothing I could do about it.

CHAPTER SEVEN

Deb usually worked days as a RN private duty nurse. A private duty nurse is a personal nurse for those wealthy or insurance-endowed enough to afford it. Deb was so empathic that her patients invariably became her friends. I know how they felt.

Since I worked nights our schedules didn't coincide except on weekends. We didn't mind as we believed a little absence made the heart grow fonder.

One morning I was alone in our Bedford Street apartment in the West Village. The words were not coming. I stared at a blank page for hours.

Maybe a jog. I loved jogging but on my rickety knees it was not such a great idea. I had to, though, I had to move, to sweat.

Once outside, I jogged down 7th Avenue to Houston then headed east. Around Mercer the idea of a Yonah Schimmel sweet potato knish popped into my head. I repressed the thought and moved north on Lafayette. I loped up to 14th Street and cruised west. I made it to 9th Avenue and 14th Street when I stopped. I walked a block or so shaking off the mile and a half workout, feeling strong, the left knee only half-threatening to collapse.

Without a conflicting thought I dipped down into the subway station on the south side of the street, slipped a token into the slot and waited on the platform with the other gray New Yorkers for the

A-train. It soon came barreling into the station. We clattered under the business district, downtown Brooklyn, the chaos of Flatbush and despair of East New York, and finally burst into the daylight of Rockaway, Queens. The train stopped at a station with a big turquoise AQUEDUCT RACE TRACK sign swinging from rusty chains connected to a flimsy corrugated overhang.

I glanced at my watch. 11 a.m. Racing didn't begin for two hours. I walked down the slanted asphalt walkway toward the general admission gates. My phone buzzed but I ignored it. A lone elderly woman in a green parka sat in a Plexiglas-enclosed kiosk working on the Daily News crossword puzzle. She looked up as I approached, flecks of pink lipstick bunched in the corners of her mouth.

"Excuse me," I said. I hated that I began so many sentences with excuse me. "Can you please direct me to the stable area?"

"You have business there?" she asked.

"I'm looking for a job on the backstretch."

"You need an appointment with a specific trainer."

"I appreciate that, ma'am," I said with a self-effacing grin. "But I couldn't help notice that 32 across, a hoopster or passport devotee, might be "globetrotter". She glanced down at the puzzle. Nodded slightly. Smiled. She wasn't so bad when she smiled.

"Walk around the parking lot," she said. "After you pass the east entrance you'll see a sign with an arrow saying Track Security. They won't let you in anyway."

"Thank you, ma'am. And have a nice day." For a moment the Plexi- glass evaporated.

It took a couple of minutes to negotiate the walk. As I did I stared up at the imposing gray Aqueduct grandstand. This is where it all began, the place which held so much promise, the womb, which became a cold and broken place, the world.

I made it to track security. A fat man in a beige Pinkerton's security outfit with a toothpick hanging out of his meaty lips looked up from a Racing Form. I got dizzy at the sight of it.

"Can I help you?" he asked.

"Yes. My name is Sid Rubin. I'm a writer. I'm working on an

article for Horse and Rider magazine. It would be helpful if I could take a quick tour of the stable area."

"You'll have to see marketing," he said. "Make an appointment. Someone from their office has to go with you." I nodded and walked away. I didn't have the strength to argue. I knew what I had to do.

CHAPTER EIGHT

That night Deb and I went to The Palm on 45th Street for dinner. It is about the last place we would normally go on our limited budget. I tried not to think of the number of taxi fares needed to pay for this extravagance. But it was a tradition. We always went on birthdays. Tonight we were celebrating my 41st. I had a birthday coupon that took twenty bucks off the tab. We sat silently waiting for our steak, five pound lobster, half and half, creamed spinach, and sautéed mushrooms. Normally Deb and I had a lot to chat about. Tonight I felt like a liar and cheat because of my visit to the track. It was not my motivation that bothered me, nor the act itself. My concern was what Deb would think.

The half and half arrived: a mountain of perfectly deep fried thin-cut potatoes and breaded onions. It is bad etiquette to use a fork to eat this. The greasier the fingers, the more the enjoyment. We concentrated on eating. I kept a wary eye on Deb making sure she didn't exceed her fair share. I couldn't believe my pettiness. I closed my eyes asking for God's will to be done. I suddenly opened them terrified that while I had been meditating Deb had gorged. She was staring at me.

"What's the matter, not hungry?" I reached over and speared a huge mound of the divine concoction, dipped it in ketchup and ladled it into my mouth.

"There's something you're not telling me," she said. "I can feel it."

"What are you talking about?"

"Sid, I've been with you for five years, six months, two days, six hours" - - she glanced at her watch – "and forty-two seconds. Make that forty-three. I can tell when my man has something on his mind."

I could have invoked the Dinkins Rule. David Dinkins was a barely competent former New York City Mayor who once told the press, "I don't want to talk about it" when a sensitive question was raised. Deb and I had this agreement that if one of us didn't want to talk about something we could invoke The Dinkins Rule and the subject couldn't be brought up for 24 hours. It was amazing how many issues became irrelevant when stored on ice for 24 hours. This was my birthday. It seemed sacred. I was sharing it with my wife. I wanted to enjoy my lobster in complete peace.

"Honey," I said. "I do have a few things on my mind. But can we talk about it tomorrow?"

Her eyes narrowed into slits. "Are you invoking The Dinkins Rule?"

"No, honey I don't need a formal ruling. Let's just enjoy our dinner and celebrate this festive occasion." It sounded like I was talking to my mother, with lying and evasion of responsibility in word and emotion.

"Oh, okay Sid, let's be festive."

I nodded and grabbed another lump of half and half and chomped away. "How's that patient you're taking care of?" I asked in an effort to change the subject.

Deb sighed. "She's an older woman in her nineties. Sweet lady. Lucid but falling apart. Kidneys, heart, anything can go. My talents, such as they are, are sort of wasted. The woman would be just as happy in a hospice. It's not nursing in the truest sense. Where were you today?"

"Today?" I said.

"Yes. This afternoon. I called you but you didn't call back."

"Oh. I - -" Out of the corner of my eye I saw our waiter

approaching, carrying a tray that bowed him into an interesting yoga position.

"Honey the food's here."

"Where were you?"

"That's it. I'm invoking The Dinkins Rule."

"On your birthday?" Deb shook her head.

"Hey. You know better."

A key proviso of The Dinkins Rule is that the other person must accept the invocation without rancor. Deb immediately got it.

"You're right. I love you, Sid." She leaned across the table. We kissed. We couldn't make it a long one. If we did, we'd permanently injure our waiter.

CHAPTER NINE

Deb acted in the spirit of The Dinkins Rule until later that night. During lovemaking she insisted I put on a rubber. At the moment of her request I was not in the mood for debate. Her timing was odd as we had been having unprotected sex for months, the unspoken agreement to try to have a child. Afterwards we were lying on our backs, thinking separate thoughts.

"Hey," I said.

"Hey."

"You hungry?"

"Hungry? I just consumed five thousand calories of The Palm's best."

"I thought maybe dessert."

"You had dessert."

Dessert was the birthday cupcake with a candle brought to our table by a scowling busboy. The birthday cupcake embarrassed me and Deb knew it and took great delight in it.

"It was a little cupcake," I said.

"Sid, I'm not the refrigerator monitor. You want to give yourself a heart attack, go ahead."

"How about a kiss?" There was a pause before she leaned over and planted a perfunctory peck on my lips. Her perfume was musky with sweat and sex. I suddenly couldn't take it.

"I was at the track today. That's where I was when you called."

She regarded me coolly. Without a word, she got up and put on her bathrobe. If she smoked she would have lit three. She returned to the bed and sat on the far corner, as far from me as possible.

"Did I hear you correctly?" she asked.

"I was at the track. Yeah. But there's more to it."

"Have you told Tony about this?"

"No. You're the first."

"I think you should talk to him." Deb thought Tony, my GA sponsor, was God. I did too, except I didn't think God was quite so intelligent.

"I'll talk to him tomorrow."

"Why did you tell me first?"

"I could feel you pulling away. I wanted to be honest."

"This is a big deal, Sid. It's like if I had a crack habit and went for a stroll on Bruckner Boulevard."

"I had business at the track."

"Really."

"Yeah. I think about my brother all the time. Everybody has forgotten him. If I don't find him nobody will. I have to go to the track to do this."

"Why?"

"There's something about the disappearance that has to have an explanation. Either he was kidnapped or it's a plot or a gambling scam or something. No one vanishes during the running of a horse race. By going to the track I can get the juices flowing."

"Sid, he disappeared in California. What good is going to Aqueduct?"

"I think, well, just by being close to security and the stable area and the sounds."

"What happened?"

"They wouldn't let me in. I have to make an appointment."

"How did you feel about being there?"

"Amazed. I was watching for feelings of desire. They were non-existent."

"It's a miracle! You're the first completely cured gambler."

"I didn't say that. Just that I know who I am. I love you and I am grateful for my life."

"I wonder," Deb said. "I wonder." A ball of hostility filled me like a poisoned balloon.

"Don't wonder too much," I said, "when I tell you I'm thinking of going to California. As it turns out you're right. Going to Aqueduct won't help. I need to go where it happened. I have a place to stay, too. A nice motel called The Surf."

"Please call Tony, Sid. Now. Call him before you throw your life away."

"I'm going to find my brother. That's all this is about."

"Is it, Sid? Is it?"

CHAPTER TEN

When I awoke Debra had gone to work. I had an emotional hangover. It felt as if I had threatened to abandon her. My trip to the track seemed a desecration, my plan to find my brother absurd.

After two cups of coffee I called my sponsor. He could see me. I dressed and strolled across 9th Street and up 3rd Avenue to his Kips Bay tenement. By the time I climbed six flights of stairs I was wheezing. He came to the door holding his naked three year old daughter in his arms.

"Hey dude," he said, ushering me into his tiny studio. Tony was a computer whiz and the Unabomber would have been comfortable in his work space. Wires, computers, motherboards, screens, and NASA-like looking contraptions were lined up floor to ceiling.

"How about a Diet Coke?" he offered.

"Sure," I said. Tony had substituted Diet Coke for his beverage of choice, Dewar's Scotch. He put away upwards of ten cans a day. I went to the fridge to get one and returned to sit on the couch across from him. His daughter was still in his arms.

"Lizzy, say hi to Sid," Tony commanded. She stuck her hand in her mouth and pulled away. Her little bare ass stared me full in the face. Shouldn't she be dressed, I thought? Couldn't he get into some kind of trouble?

"So dude, you're looking well," he said.

"You too, Tony, you too. Daughter's really growing."

"Oh yeah, she's a big girl." Tony grabbed her by the ankles and lifted her upside down into the air. I was sure the lower half of her body would snap off like a Lego but all the kid did was scream with delight.

When order was restored he asked, "So what brings you by, dude?"

"My love and regard for you," I said.

"Well isn't that nice," Tony said. "I wouldn't have guessed it."

"It would be nice if that's the only reason I came over, wouldn't it?"

"The hell it would," he said. "I don't let crazy people in my house."

"I went to the track yesterday," I said as casually as possible.

"Of all places."

"Not to gamble."

"That's a relief."

"To check out the backstretch. I felt a need to find my brother."

"Your brother?"

"Yeah," I said. "You seem surprised."

"Your brother has disappeared. Do you have investigative powers of which I'm unaware?"

"I'm his brother."

"My brother's a pulmonary surgeon but you won't find me dipping an endoscope down somebody's throat."

"The parallel would be if I tried to become a jockey."

"No, we're talking about irrational behavior," he said. "What makes you think you can succeed where more qualified people haven't?"

"My brother appears to me in dreams. I really believe he's alive. I'm not sure the others do."

"So belief will fuel your investigation."

"That's important."

"I'm not saying it's not, dude. Came to believe a power great than ourselves will return us to sanity. The Second Step. I'm not one to knock belief. Just nutty belief systems. What does your higher power think about your half-brained scheme?"

"I haven't asked."

"He doesn't work on weekends?"

"Maybe I should pray and meditate on this," I said.

"Or not. That's your business. How's Debra?"

"She wanted me to talk to you. She's pretty upset over my plan."

"She's a good woman. And she loves you."

"Go figure," I said.

His daughter swiveled around to face me, her innocent blue eyes bored a hole through me. I tried to focus on the eyes and not the little button breasts or the hairless, smooth vagina.

"Look," he continued, "I know you love your brother and you want to help. Is there another way to do this besides making yourself so vulnerable?"

"I don't think so. I've always been a coward. This is my chance to be fearless."

"Going to the racetrack is fearless?"

"Are you saying there's no chance I can find my brother?"

"I'd say there's a better chance you can grow a peach out of your ass."

"So what do I do?"

"Thirty meetings in thirty days. You haven't been going much, have you?"

"No."

"I'll go with you tonight. That meeting over on 24th and 2nd, there's this beautiful babe I'd love to fuck. She's from England. Too bad she's a newcomer." This sounded especially crass articulated in front of his daughter.

"We'll go. Tonight. Okay, dude?"

I nodded and got to my feet.

"Say goodbye to Sid, Lizzy." She stuck her tongue out, blew and made a farting sound. She didn't think much of my plan either.

34

CHAPTER ELEVEN

Once I was back outside the depression hit. Not even a pastrami on rye with Russian and coleslaw at the Second Avenue Deli could restore my sense of well being. Did my sponsor have what I wanted? A cruddy little apartment and a naked baby after twelve years of sobriety? What was I thinking, trying to make a baby with Debra. I should have thanked her for making me wear a rubber.

My impulse to find my brother was heroic. Yet my wife was fearful and sent me to my sponsor who told me to go to more meetings. The Twelve Step programs are littered with fools who substitute one crutch for another, and one that isn't nearly as enjoyable as the original.

Why was I in New York City? For a wife who thought I was an emotional cripple? A writing career that was going nowhere? A boring, dangerous cab driving job? An apartment that had a nice view of an overflowing dumpster? Nothing made sense.

I got to the cab garage at about 3:30, got lucky, and was assigned a good cab. When I say "good" I mean the steering wheel was attached, the brakes worked, and there was no overwhelming stench of urine or fecal matter.

By 6:30 I was in a mindless rhythm of pre-programmed maneuvers according to lights and traffic. The fares were coming one after the other. In spite of the constant business the ennui descended like the fog into which my brother disappeared.

I dipped into the Market Dinner on 37th and 9th for a cup of coffee and one of their superb glazed donuts. A late edition New York Post was on the counter. I turned to the Sports Section. The Knicks were playing badly, the Giants and Jets floundering. I flipped past stories about Joe Torre, Roger Clemens, George Steinbrenner, marlin fishing, bowling and there it was: THE RACING PAGE. Results. Selections. Charts. I hadn't looked at it for better than two years. I flicked by it like it was electrified.

I hated that I couldn't read it. This was crazy. I was a great handicapper. It was when the beer hit that I had the problems. But that was a long time ago when the fear ruled and that was before the epiphanies and the knowledge and when I was able to see into the game past the fear and numbers and what seemed to be and…I clamped my hands over my ears in an attempt to silence this maddening dialogue. The Serenity Prayer popped into my head like a mantra: "God, Grant Me The Serenity To Accept The Things I Cannot Change, The Courage To Change The Things I Can, and The Wisdom To Know The Difference." Every time I thought of the Serenity Prayer it meant something new and different. Today the word Serenity stood out as if I had heard it for the first time. That's what this whole life-thing was about, right? Serenity?

Back in the cab I picked up a lovely young couple at the Stanhope Hotel at 81st and 5th. They were going to theater to see "The Producers". As I glanced at their blond-haired heads in the rear view I wondered if they would get the satire or snap off a Zig Heil. As we started talking, I realized I had stereotyped them badly. They were actually smart, good kids from Indiana, names of Kenny and Kelly. They met at the Corn Festival outside Muncie where she was the reigning Kernel Queen. They both went to Indiana and Kenny actually played ball for Coach Bobby Knight during the farewell season. He told me Knight was a great guy and he only saw Coach hit two players and choke a third.

"But they deserved it," Kenny said, "running their gangsta stuff, you know?"

"I sure do," I said. "I was a big fan of Coach Knight. Still am."

"He was my hero," Kenny said dreamily.

"Do you like driving the cab?" asked the Kernel Queen. Her teeth glistened like diamonds. I wanted to ask, do you like monkey nuts in your morning granola?

"It's a job," I said.

"I've always wanted to drive a cab," Kenny said. "I just think it would be the coolest thing." Without giving it a second thought I wheeled the cab over to the east side of 58th and 5th.

"It's your big chance, Kenny." I got out and held the door open. His jaw was hanging like Coach Knight just admitted a sexual preference for Airedales.

"No shit no shit no shit," said Kenny.

I watched him get behind the wheel and grip it until his knuckles were popping out of his hands. I got into the backseat with Kelly. I didn't have to tell Kenny to take it slow because traffic was a bear.

He did pretty well except for the right turn on 47th when he nearly sheared the arm off a traffic cop. By the time we got to the theatre at 7:55, Kelly and I were friends. She insisted Debra and I come out for Christmas.

The looks on the faces of the theatergoers as the fare jumped out of the back of the cab, got paid by the cabbie who then walked off with the fare's date as the fare got into the front and drove off, was priceless. The $20 bill Kenny gave me for the trip wasn't bad either.

CHAPTER TWELVE

Debra's parents were coming for dinner. This meant storing my card-table desk, chair and other writing items in a closet so four people could eat at the same time. As her parents were big drinkers I also had to go to the liquor store to buy a bottle of Absolut, their vodka of choice. Luckily none of my AA chums were around to witness the purchase.

Deb grew up in Mt. Vernon, a city just north of New York City. Her mom had always been a housewife. Dad owned and still ran an air- conditioning and heating store. I worked in the store for two weeks one summer and still have nightmares thinking about trying to find poorly inventoried items in a dark, dank warehouse.

Deb is a great cook and tonight it was spaghetti, turkey meatballs, and a vegetarian eggplant casserole. Her mom is famous for not eating. Few people have seen her ingest anything other than fiber cookies and jello, except on special occasions, like tonight. There was a lot of pressure on Deb.

I lugged the Formica dining room table into the living room and arranged four Samsonite chairs around it. My days as a Sardi's busboy came in handy and I made little napkin crowns and placed them on the dinner plates. We didn't have four of everything and so the forks and salad bowls were mismatched. I was thrilled that everything was functional. Deb entered a deep fugue state about three hours before the folks arrived and said not a word the entire time.

They arrived on the dot of six. Mom was thin, small, withered, yet vital. At six feet dad towered over her. Everything about him was gray and puffy.

"Hello, Sidney," mom said. No one had called me Sidney since the lady at the DMV three years before. We hugged, she gave me a perfunctory peck on the cheek and swept into the apartment with a "charming, charming, look what you've gone through for us". Dad grasped me on both arms and beamed. "Good to see you buddy." I involuntarily flexed my biceps.

There was nowhere to sit except the table so cocktails were served where we would be eating. They liked their booze straight and on the rocks.

"Good," said dad, smacking his lips. "Absolut?"

"Absolutely, Mr. Langer." I wouldn't dare call him Phil.

"Come in and join us, honey," mom called to Debra. Debra walked out, wiping her hands on a napkin. A smile that could have been surgically implanted creased her unwilling face. She sat more erect than I had ever seen her. Statue like. She and I sipped cranberry juice.

"We found a parking space right out front," beamed dad.

"That's a miracle," I said. I was sure he had parked in a poorly-marked tow away zone but I didn't have the energy to check.

"The apartment is lovely, dear," said mom.

"Hope you have a shoe horn so I can get out," laughed dad, sucking away at the vodka. Within a minute, they were both ready for refills. Unlike true alcoholics, Deb's parents got happier the more they drank. I'd seen no evidence of the alcohol induced insanity that characterizes other people's drinking, like mine.

"So how's the writing going, Sidney," asked mom.

"It's going okay. Working on a screenplay, you know."

"We worry about you driving that cab," said dad. I was about to tell them not to worry, the passengers are driving these days. But a glance from Deb stopped me.

"You know, Sid, I can use you in the store. You were a great inventory clerk. Rudy and Sal still talk about you. I know it's not something a college grad plans to do but it's good steady work. And I'm not going to be a kid forever!" He laughed and slugged more Absolut.

"I appreciate that, Mr. Langer. And it's great to know it's there."

Dinner went well. Debra's paralysis abated and the four of us engaged in discussions ranging from AIDS, the insanity of President Bush, the cost of chicken, used cars, movies and the amount of BTU's necessary for a proper running window air conditioning unit. Deb's pasta and eggplant casseroles were huge hits. Mom had seconds.

After the folks left, about two hours after they arrived, we felt good. When I heard their car start up and knew it hadn't been towed the evening could be judged a success. It's only when we got into bed and Deb asked me to seriously consider working for dad that I felt the darkness closing in.

CHAPTER THIRTEEN

In the beginning God created luck. You've got to have it or you don't exist. Luck is not the meeting of opportunity and preparation. It's energy, that's all, borne of interest and ability. I haven't been lucky. Maybe not even meeting Debra was lucky. In falling in love and marrying her I achieved a dependency. I sublimated a creative side of myself in pleasing her. She was my wife, my mother. So much energy was bound up in pretending to be a writer and dutiful husband that none was available for luck.

I needed to free the energy. This may have had something to do with finding my brother. I was ten when he was born. My speed-ridden mother could not believe she was pregnant. She had her hands full with me. The last thing she wanted was another kid. My father, well, he was working so hard at boozing it up and keeping his family together I'm not sure he noticed. It was a tough pregnancy. Mom more or less remained in bed the entire time. When John was born I felt I lost something. My parents' attention was on him. When I was fourteen my brother developed an extreme attachment. He idolized me. The more he expressed his love, the more I turned off.

By the time I was sixteen I hated him. When I baby sat, which was often, I ignored him. He was a useless little joke, little being the operative word. He was physically small. When I went away to college I did so feeling that I was leaving behind an aberration.

I got into horse race handicapping and my life started to go down the tubes. When I was twenty-six John reached out to me, told me that whenever I needed him he would be there. He sent me money a couple of times, then realized I was gambling it away. By the time he graduated from college I was on my way to a richly deserved obscurity. When I came home at Thanksgiving all I could talk about was how close I was to making it at the races. He saw it destroying me. He was still short and slight, maybe 100 pounds dripping wet.

Out of the blue he went to jockey school in Santa Fe, New Mexico to learn about race riding. His only prior experience with a horse was a mechanical pony outside the local Walgreen's. The family thought he had lost his mind and everybody else thought he was too old. After he graduated he rode at small racetracks in Northern California and New Mexico, picking up valuable riding experience. He met a former jockey, a Panamanian named Gustavo Clemente, who mentored him and became his agent.

Clemente took John to Panama, the plan being that John would learn about riding at the rough and tumble Central American racetracks before plying his trade in the States. Within ten months John was the leading rider at the top Panamanian track. When John and I talked all I wanted was to get horse tips, not that any bookie I knew would take action on a racetrack in Panama.

John returned to the USA about the time I moved into a flophouse on the Bowery. He came to Belmont as an unknown seven pound apprentice rider. His solid Panamanian reputation mattered little in the States.

Every time he saw me I could feel his love. I could not believe my baby brother was a full time jockey. I'd steer the conversation around to horses he was riding, trying to get information. He repeatedly told me that I had as much chance at predicting the winner as he did. One day Clemente told me that if I didn't stop bothering John he would kill me.

Shortly thereafter Clemente took John to Southern California. Clemente probably figured that even though John was just a plane ride away, I'd never spend $400 on a ticket when I could bet it on a horse. I met Debra about six months after John left for California.

John and I had done okay in the intervening two years.

CHAPTER FOURTEEN

Once I made the decision to go to California a frostiness settled in between Deb and I. One night I tried to make love to her and she got up, dressed and left the apartment. I was left to jerk off in the dark, wondering where she was.

I got a reservation on a new airline that offered cheap flights and was the only airline still serving food in coach. I bought a one-way ticket.

I was in my writing nook one morning when Debra walked in. She pulled up a Samsonite and glanced at the empty screen.

"Haven't been doing too much writing," she said.

"I'm blocked."

"Thinking about your trip?"

"Maybe."

"I'm disappointed you didn't talk to me more about your intentions."

"You know what I have to do, Deb."

"There's more to it."

"Like what?"

"Like we have a good life. I know at times it feels pointless. That's the nature of recovery, to plateau and grow. Don't mistake a bump in the road for a dead end."

"I'm going to find out what happened to my brother." This

had become my mantra.

"Don't blow it, Sid," she said.

"Yeah, sure."

"Not to mention that we're married."

"I know that."

"And part of me feels like you're abandoning me." Her lower lip quivered and she started to cry. I watched as she put her pretty little head into her hands. Sobs wracked her shoulders. Mascara blackened tears dropped onto her white nurse's pants. As they fell on the fabric, dark wetness spread in all directions.

I turned off the computer, went to her, put my arms around her.

"Don't touch me," she snarled. "You're a selfish bastard. Don't you get it, hasn't any of your 12-Step work clued you to the fact that the biggest problem in your life is your self-obsession? What **you** want and when **you** want it? This whole thing makes me sick." She stormed into the bathroom and slammed the door.

I sat at my writing table for another few minutes. My self-pity took the form of blaming myself for hurting Deb, the most precious person in my life. It was proof that I was a scumbag.

I went to the deli in Sheridan Square and in the back I stared at the beer. Thank God they didn't have Labatt's, my favorite brew. I stared at the Bud, Coors, Heineken, Fosters, mentally recollecting the subtle differences of each beer's high. I opened the case, put my hand on a St. Paulie Girl. I pulled one out and cradled it.

"Hey, bro, you gonna buy it or fuck it?" asked the cashier. His words snapped me back to my senses. I smiled, put the bottle back, and bought a bag of pork rinds.

Munching away I returned home. When I got there, Deb was gone. Her small suitcase was missing from the corner of the closet. There was no note.

For a few hours, I sat in the armchair by the phone, wishing there was someone I wanted to call, hoping Deb would call me. A crying jag ensued but I stopped the second I realized I was crying for myself. I wanted MY SELF to see how sad I WAS.

The thought crossed my mind: what would I have done if

Deb wanted to go with me? She could do that, her job gave her flexibility.

I realized with a start how badly I wanted to do this myself.

CHAPTER FIFTEEN

I left late one night carrying a small flight bag. I glanced one last time at the table where Deb and I spent hours reading the papers and sharing breakfasts. Now it was empty.

It troubled me that I thought of the $2,000 in my pocket as a stake and not money I had to support myself on the journey to find my brother. Gamblers think of money as a stake, not normal people. In an effort to save dough I took the A train to the airport and a shuttle bus to the terminal.

My redeye coach seat was on the aisle. The fact people bumped into my elbow repeatedly without apologizing reminded me how evolved I would be if I could get beyond the homicidal urge to kill them. I busied myself reading a trashy novel and gazing across the aisle at a pretty young woman whose belly shirt had risen up under her bra as she sprawled on her back across three seats, one arm thrown over her eyes in a fitful sleep.

The attendants remembered to make my Coke easy ice and as I sipped I felt good. I was on a plane bound for California. I was incipient danger, the kernel of paradise. I dozed off for a few minutes.

When I woke a lovely dish of macaroni and a meat like substance was in front of me. The airline was as good as their word. As I ate I thought of LA. I had been studying maps of LA for about a month. I had a pretty good idea of the city in my mind.

After I finished eating, I noticed my sleeping, matronly seatmate had left her brownie uneaten. The more I tried to ignore the brownie the more I obsessed on it. I gauged how deeply the woman slept by softly calling "hello, hello", then louder. When I was certain she was out, I reached and gently lifted the brownie from the tray. Without opening her eyes, she grabbed my wrist in a vice grip.

"Are you insane?" she hissed. She was a fat old woman with thin lips, eyebrows, nose, and ears. If her body and face were reversed it would have been a real plus,

"I'm so sorry," I said. "I thought you were asleep. They were going to take away the tray and well, I thought…"

"Don't bullshit a bullshitter," she growled. "They never take the tray when there's food left without asking."

"I don't think that's true," I said lamely.

"One hundred and thirty six thousand miles I flew last year. My girls, Siamese twins, were surgically separated in March. It's too bad Myra chose to live in Miami and Edith in LA."

"I'd have thought they'd want to remain together."

"Twenty seven years was enough." I watched as she pushed the overhead call button.

"Why'd you do that?" I asked.

"Because you're a thief. You might as well try to hijack the whole plane. You're capable of that, aren't you?"

"Yeah," I said, "and you're my first hostage, you fat witch. I only wonder how much I'd have to pay them to take you back."

"You'll be sorry you said that, sonny."

An Asian attendant appeared. My seatmate claimed I tried to steal her brownie, take her hostage and hijack the plane. The attendant had trouble getting her mind around how the brownie and hijack plot were related. Fortunately, my seatmate was such a raving lunatic that the solution was to move me to another seat in the back and not incarcerate me on air piracy charges.

I reflected on the incident and wondered how a man in my condition could be deluded enough to think he could help anybody, much less someone who had vanished from the face of the earth.

CHAPTER SIXTEEN

I rented a red Neon at the Budget Car Rental at LAX. Budget may charge as much as Hertz and Avis but because of the name it feels like you're getting a deal. The car had an unfortunate tendency to squirt backward when in reverse, whether or not my foot was on the gas pedal. But it was only $145 a week and I had driven cabs that were worse. The color troubled me for my mother had predicted that I would die in a red car.

The little rental had quite a bit of pep for a 4 cylinder cookie cutter. This power proved irrelevant for I was soon trapped in the longest and most horrifying traffic jam I had ever seen. I had time to familiarize myself with the LA radio stations and was able to find one passable song, "Cheap Sunglasses" by ZZ Top, in over an hour. I ended up listening to classical music, which was never thrilling but satisfying, sort of like my sober, married life in New York.

By the time I exited the 405 at Wilshire and headed east, I had no idea where I was. After I drove for a few miles I was startled to see La Cienega Boulevard, a street I noticed just outside the airport. It meant the 405 veered west as it curved into the San Fernando Valley.

I went south on La Cienega. My eye was caught by a motel. I could not believe it. It was the motel from the postcards I had been getting in New York. The one with a purple Surf sign and beneath a blue ocean and a couple of green palm trees. Purple neon script attached to the ocean's edge said weekly rates were available. I pulled into the lot and went into the lobby. Without trying to drive a bargain with the female Indian room clerk who weighed about 27 pounds, most of it in the largest nose I had ever seen, I got a nice room in back for $125 a week.

"We have the HBO too, sir," she said proudly, sipping at a can of Slimfast. If I had any doubts about The Surf they were erased by knowing I would be able to watch "The Sopranos", "Curb your Enthusiasm", and the Saturday Night Fights on HBO. The room was clean, spare, and unadorned by any attempt at interior decorating save for a Surf Motel Sign mounted over the bed identical to the sign at the motel entrance. The "weekly rates available" script peeked through several layers of peach enamel.

I checked my watch. Just after 9 A.M. The track opened in two hours. I got out my stake — I mean the money I had to support this journey — and counted it. Just under $2,000. I flicked on the TV using a greasy remote. A Steven Segal movie was on HBO. Perfect. As I watched Segal single-handedly maim the army of a small country, I fell into a deep sleep. In my dream I was tapped out. I was driving the cab and terrified I had no money. My brother was in the rearview wearing cerise jockey silks.

I woke up bathed in sweat. I took a shower and changed my clothes. The Indian clerk had no idea where I could get a good breakfast. I got into the Neon and headed south on La Cienega. I stopped into a Pollo Loco and got a chicken bowl which wasn't half bad.

I made it to Hollywood Park just before 1 PM. As I pulled into the parking lot off Prairie Avenue I gaped at the imposing green and gray structure. The roar of planes flying overhead deafened me. I parked the car and headed toward the track entrance.

CHAPTER SEVENTEEN

I bought a program and went up a couple of escalators to the second floor of the grandstand. It was a weekday crowd, sparse and mostly male, and I felt as if I was in the Third World or maybe The Fourth.

Hollywood Park reminded me of Aqueduct as far as racetracks went. Not much aesthetically pleasing. From the grey walls to the scuffed coat of tan paint on the asphalt, Hollywood Park felt like a track whose time had come and gone.

I went outside and chose the seat covered with the least amount of bird shit. My section overlooked the finished line. The infield was landscaped nicely with good sized lawns. A kidney shaped lake curved around a long tote board. A huge big screen TV to the side of the tote board featured a big bottle of Jack Daniels and the words, "Our Benevolent Sponsor" underneath. Pink flamingos swirled through grey water so slowly that for a few minutes I was not certain they were real.

What captivated me was the oval itself – the racetrack. My eyes made a slow counter-clockwise consideration of it from finish line to finish line. This was the place where it happened. Ground zero.

The horses for the first race came onto the track. My program told me they were bottom of the barrel $10,000 claimers. I checked out the horses, trainers and jockeys. I recognized most of the jockeys and trainers but few of the horses.

I rifled through the program seeing if Robert Lemmons had a horse running. Lemmons was the trainer of Princess Bride, the horse that vanished. He had a horse going in the last race. I made a mental note to get down to the paddock and check him out.

I strolled to a concession stand and got an orange soda. A security guard in a green jacket stood nearby. He was an older guy, ramrod straight and wiry, probably a former military man. His .9mm revolver was slung low on his waist like a gunslinger's.

"Hi," I said.

"Hi," he said.

"It's my first time at Hollywood Park. Nice track you have here."

"Thanks. Where are you from?"

"New York. Out for a vacation."

"Enjoy yourself."

"How can I not?" I smiled. "It's the racetrack."

He smiled back. "Yeah, the racetrack." I slugged back a big hit of orange soda.

"It's really something what happened a few months ago."

"What's that?"

"You know, that horse and jockey disappearing." A curtain came down over his eyes.

"Yeah," he said.

"Can you imagine that happening?"

"Look," he said, "we don't talk about that anymore. Good luck in your stay." He tipped his cap and walked away.

I asked the counter girl where the Security Office was located. She directed me to a stairwell which I took down into the bowels of the building. I walked along a narrow corridor lined with pipes and past offices housing Marketing, Administration, Stewards, Racing Secretary, and finally Security. I pushed open a swinging door to discover four green-jacketed officers sitting around a battered table on which was arrayed a huge box of donuts, an igloo cooler, and a jar of Cremora. Unlike the Security guard upstairs three of the officers were fat old men. The fourth was a woman, younger but just as large.

"Hey," I said. "Where do I report a lost wallet?"

They looked at one another as if to see who would be forced to get off his ass and miss a turn at the donuts. One finally waddled up to the counter. A small badge on his jacket said Henry Farmer.

"You'll have to fill out a form," he said. As he went through piles of paper hanging out of a drawer I took in the office. Everything about it felt unprofessional.

"Hey Homer," he called to another guard. "You know where those lost and found forms are?"

Homer looked up from a glazed donut. "Should be in that pile, Harry."

"Where'd you lose it?" asked Henry.

"Ah, don't worry about it," I said. "It's not that big of a deal." As I walked out I felt an urge to glance back. Henry was staring at me and he had a walkie-talkie in his hand.

CHAPTER EIGHTEEN

While in the basement I stopped in a cavernous restroom. There must have been forty urinals lined up under a paint-chipped wall. If everybody in the grandstand was to take a piss at the same time the place would still be half-empty. An innocent-faced janitor with a mop and bucket scrubbed the floor diligently. I walked up a flight of stairs to the main level of the grandstand. It was the era of simulcasting, or simultaneous broadcasting. Racing signals were piped in from various tracks around the country at the same time. TV sets hung all over the place.

Simulcasting meant that in addition to being able to bet on Hollywood Park horses the degenerates swirling about me could bet up to six other tracks at the same time. And they could bet earlier, too, as the East Coast races started at 9:30 a.m. Pacific Coast Time. It was almost like a full time job for the horseplayers, the only difference being that not only was there no paycheck, there was no home, clothes, car, or relationships after a couple of months at the office.

The scene was like something out of "Night Of The Living Dead". Ashen faced guys shuffled instead of walked, slouched instead of stood, listless and zombie like. Some held Racing Forms in front of them like antennae, not looking up, intuiting how to avoid bumping into the other zombies. I thought of Brownian movement, a scientific principle which explained the random motion of molecules.

It was as if someone had taken a vacuum and sucked up the energy. I wasn't sure a doctor in search of a pulse could find one. And there was something more, an apathy or withdrawal from anything resembling life. With their nondescript clothes, tattered shoes, grizzled faces, decayed teeth, greasy hair and disinterested expressions the racetrack denizens appeared to have suffered a terrible loss. I got the feeling it had nothing to do with money.

Maybe what I was witnessing was a delayed response to what happened to my brother and Princess Bride. Horseplayers are a cynical lot and nothing about the venality of human nature surprises them. But this mystery must have strained even their incredulity. In the absence of any possible explanation they had receded more deeply into themselves.

I sidled up next to a grizzled old stick of a black man who leaned against a pillar with a small styrofoam cup of coffee clutched in a gnarled hand. I wasn't sure he'd had a good meal in a month but here he was at the racetrack, holes in his shoes and a pink $3 tout sheet sticking out of his windbreaker pocket.

"You like anything today?" I asked.

He smiled, revealing a 7-10 split where teeth used to be.

"I aint' the one to be askin', palie. Ain't had a winner in a gottamn long time." It occurred to me that most Americans believe in got and not God.

"Whatever you think is more than I know," I said.

"Well, then maybe the two horse in the seventh is worth a couple of bucks."

"Thanks, buddy," I said. "I don't come to Hollywood Park too often.Were you here when that horse disappeared a few months ago?"

"Was I here? Hell, I had that horse in a pick three!" A Pick Three is a bet where you have to pick the winners of three races in a row to cash.

"No shit," I said.

"I don't shit unless I'm sittin' on a porcelain loveseat," he said. "No, that horse cost me a $133 Pick Three. There's on thousand ways to lose a race and just one way to win. Leave it to me to find the one thousand and first."

"What do you think happened?"

"To be plain with you, I don't have no clue. I'm sure there's a reasonable explanation. I know that horse was gonna win. Another trainer probably backed a van up and pulled him away." As he took a sip of java I watched his eyes dart around as if he expected to see Princess Bride appear at any moment.

I thanked him for his time. I had conversations with ten or fifteen more patrons. All of them had been scarred by the disappearance, as if they, like I, had lost a loved one.

For the rest of the day I pretty much remained glued to my seat in the grandstand. There were sprints, routes and a couple of races run on the turf course. All proceeded uneventfully. As the horses thundered down the backstretch my attention sharpened. Except for a small green gate in the middle of the backstretch that led to barns in the distance there seemed to be no way for a horse to disappear. I monitored myself carefully. I had no urge to place a bet.

Around the fifth race the skies opened and there was a brief downpour which settled into a drizzle. It was miserable and the only reason I stuck around was to get a glimpse of trainer Lemmons.

I knew of Lemmons but had never laid eyes on him. He had the reputation of being a competent but marginal trainer. A few years ago he was investigated when a horse he trained was killed with an injection of fecal matter in an insurance scam. He was exonerated. I checked out the current standings and saw he had won with just three of the thirty-three horses he had run.

With twenty minutes left before the final race I pried myself off my seat and went down to the paddock. Nearby a huge barbeque was grilling up the largest burgers and dogs I had ever seen and they smelled good. I realized I was very hungry but decided I would wait until I returned to LA to have dinner.

The paddock was well-appointed and picturesque. No matter how crummy the track the paddock is always nice. It's where the owners come before the race and where TV monitors check out the horses. The paddock at Hollywood park featured a freshly painted white ranch fence inside of which was a walking ring and a lawn manicured as well as a golf course green. I stood on an asphalt tarmac just outside the fence. Around me were pockets of lawn, floral displays, oak trees, and park benches.

Lemmons's horse was an older gelding by the name of Minor Key, the one horse. With about sixteen minutes before post an older, short man with a swizzle stick hanging out of his mouth wandered over to the part of the paddock where a wooden sign emblazoned with the number "1" hung from a pole stuck into the lawn. Lemmons wore dirty black jeans, work boots, and a western shirt unbuttoned midway to this navel revealing more hair than sprouted from his head. His eyes were half-hidden by lowered lids.

A brown-skinned woman in her 60's in a peach pastel dress with matching handbag and shoes strolled out and gave Lemmons a quick hug. She must have been the owner. I checked out the program and saw her name was Shiva Singh. My heart skipped a beat when I realized she was the owner of Princess Bride, too.

They were joined in short order by the jockey, a journeyman named Mike Orr, who had the same success as a jockey that Lemmons had as a trainer. They shook hands. In a gentlemanly gesture Orr removed his cap and bowed slightly to Mrs. Singh. The three talked about something I could not hear until the horses were brought out.

As the horses circled the walking ring I watched Lemmons give Orr instructions. Lemmons made a pushing motion with his hands and nodded in response to Orr's question. Mrs. Singh observed placidly, clutching her handbag. Minor Key didn't seem to notice or care. I glanced up at the tote board: Minor Key was 25-1. As I didn't have a Racing Form I couldn't tell whether he had a chance. From what I observed of Lemmons and his operation it probably wasn't much.

The groom stopped Minor Key in front of them. "Riders Up," boomed the voice of the walking ring official. Lemmons kneeled, placed his clasped hands under Orr's left boot and lifted him into the saddle with a practiced, quick extension of his arms. Minor Key came to life and pranced for a stride or two. Then he and the other steeds were led to the waiting ponies to follow the Marshall onto the track for the post parade.

CHAPTER NINETEEN

I picked up some Nachos "Supreme" at a Taco Bell on La Cienega and ate them in my room while watching Sports Center on ESPN. I'd hate to see what the Nachos "Regular" was like.

I ran through the events of the day but stopped when my mind could not make sense of it. The fear and mistrust at the track were tough to take.

When I went to the bathroom I got a surprise. On the toilet seat, instead of a Sani Strip were several pages of massage ads from the local counter-culture papers, While relieving myself I read them, amazed at the breadth and complexity of services offered by a bevy of gorgeous women. Apparently it was possible to have one's feet tickled, prostate probed, and ass flayed simultaneously. For a price, of course.

Ad in hand I wandered into the lobby. The Indian woman was sitting in a comfortable chair watching the movie "Charlie's Angels" on what I assumed was "the HBO". Upon seeing me she jumped to her feet.

"Mr. Rubin, good evening, sir, is everything peachy, sir?"

"Fine, ah - -"

"Mitra. You may call me Mitra."

"Ah, yes, Mitra…"

My words trailed off as we both reflexively watched the

movie. Cameron Diaz danced around in a skimpy bra and panties. I glanced down at the ads. It seemed a natural segue.

"I found these in my room." I offered the ad.

"Ah, yes, Mr. Rubin, sir, I have placed them here."

"You did?"

"Of course, sir. A man must have his needs met in order to think clearly."

Why hadn't I thought of that? Perhaps if I had received a blowjob before going to the track it all would have made sense.

"Well, I won't be requiring these services at the present. If I do I'll let you know."

"I know these girls, Mr. Rubin. Whatever you need. Clean, good girls and they arrive at The Surf instantly. No rush jobs."

"Excellent."

"Would you like a vanilla Slimfast or perhaps a strawberry Yoo Hoo before you go?" asked Mitra.

"Oh, no thank you. Maybe some other time."

"Of course, Mr. Rubin. I am always at your service. Oh yes, don't forget. After "the Charlie's Angels", "The Castaway" is playing on the HBO."

"Thanks, Mitra."

As I returned to my room I noticed I still held the ads. I placed them on my dresser. Although I preferred anonymity, Mrs. Singh seemed harmless enough.

Although I had seen "Castaway" once before, when it aired I was fully absorbed. Watching Hanks disintegrate from a soft, civilized man into a fearful primitive and then evolve into a self-sufficient survivor was meaningful. It symbolized my journey.

Although I was not yet lonely, I knew loneliness would come, and that was what almost killed me last time. I knew this time I must embrace it.

I looked around my room. There was nothing identifiable. I pulled the bottom sheet up from the bed for an instant, peered at the label on the mattress, then tucked it back under.

"Simmons," I said as I laid back down, "we are going to find out what happened to my brother."

CHAPTER TWENTY

The next morning I drove into Beverly Hills and had a cup of coffee and a corn muffin as dry as a cinder at a Starbuck's on Beverly Boulevard. While I was there Cindy Lauper wandered in, ordered a Latte and took an adjacent table. I couldn't think of anything to ask except do girls really just want to have fun so I said nothing. She never looked at me, just stared into space.

I got to the Beverly Hills Library on Crescent Drive just after ten. It didn't take me long to find the LA Times reporter of record on my brother's story was a guy named Lars Nyquist.

I checked my Thomas map guide and took Beverly Boulevard straight downtown to the Times office. There was a gradual decrease in opulence as I traveled east until by the time I passed a street called Rampart every building had bars across the windows. Wild dogs trotted the streets in packs and fences cordoned off weed and garbage strewn lots. I had inadvertently driven past The LA Times onto Skid Row.

I had never seen anything like this squalor and I had driven a cab in New York City on and off for fifteen years. This was not poverty, this was a post apocalyptic landscape of drug-addled, mutated humans in various stages of undress.

I swung back to First Street, parked, found The Times building, and spotted a burly security guard at a desk just inside revolving doors. I waited until a shapely female bustled past and eased behind her, shielded by her surgery swelled breasts.

Nyquist worked in the back of the feature department, cubicle 137B to be exact. When I got there he was leaning back in an office chair playing computer basketball.

"Mr. Nyquist?"

"Oh, hello," he said. My appearance didn't seem to be a surprise.

"My name is Sid Rubin," I said. "I'm the brother of John Rubin, the jockey who disappeared. You covered the story for the Times."

"I did, yes I did, good to meet you, Sid." He brought the chair forward and extended a hand. "One day I'll get the Clippers to win," nodding at the video game. A shock of sandy blonde hair framed his scholarly, young, bespectacled face. His hand felt like paraffin.

"I suppose you're here to ask about your brother," he said. A flatness in his voice reminded me of something I couldn't place.

"Yes, exactly," I said.

"Have you eaten?" he asked. "I know a place that serves great pancakes." He grabbed a coat from a hook on the wall and led me out of the office.

We walked five or six blocks down Figueroa in virtual silence to an eatery called The Pantry. We opted for a couple of seats at the counter and were thus able to avoid standing on the long line of corpulent businessmen that snaked down the street. Two cups of black coffee were slapped onto the counter like inoculations.

"Where are you from, Sid?" asked Nyquist.

"New York City."

"Of course, John was from New York. In reverse order, do you like California? When did you arrive? What kind of car are you renting? Do you like pastry?"

The barrage of questions was delivered without pause in the same monotone. I noticed a fresh scar that ran across his right temple just to the right of his eyebrow. It appeared six or seven stitches had been recently removed.

"Prune Danish, a Neon, recently, yes." An elderly waiter appeared and stared at us. I asked for a couple of menus. He jerked his head at a blackboard behind him upon which was written the fare. I asked for a minute or two. He glared at me and shuffled away.

"That's good, Sid, because we have to appreciate what we have. There isn't room for dissent, not here at the Pantry, anyway. Why, when a horse and rider just vanish my mother has no room for dresses in her closet. In reverse order, do you like maple syrup with your pancakes? Where do we go when we yawn or sneeze? What's your favorite Stones song? Does the yak have a mating call?"

"Yes, Brown Sugar, limbo, and who doesn't. Are you feeling okay, Mr. Nyquist?"

"Oh yes, I am fine. I am very, very well." He fingered the scar. "I was agitated when they took me in but now I am fine. I will be leaving the Times tomorrow to visit my family in Oslo."

CHAPTER TWENTY - ONE

My experience with Nyquist was disconcerting. The guy was disoriented and of no help whatsoever. The scar on his forehead made me think he had a lobotomy.

The next two days Hollywood Park was shuttered. I drove around LA and the surrounding freeways trying to get a sense of the territory. The division between haves and have-nots confronted me at every turn. I drove into the hills north of Sunset Boulevard and observed miles and miles of palatial mansions worth millions. In East LA and to the south were shacks supported by nothing other than tin and aluminum and which sprouted from the earth like weeds. Almost everywhere outside of Beverly Hills people spoke Spanish or English with Spanish accents. I wondered if Los Angelenos were aware they were rapidly becoming Jalisco north.

I called Debra and my sponsor. No answer. I left no messages. I felt the need for a connection. Why did I need someone to give me security? I wished I was a Navy Seal, trained and independent.

In lieu of military training I watched HBO. Mitra and I discussed the merits of older and younger actresses. She thought highly of Meryl Streep and I went with Jennifer Garner. Garner's performance in *Daredevil* was one of the best ever.

I ate meals in my room and mapped out strategy. I calculated that my now $1,600 stake might last a couple of months if I was frugal. That meant no fries and milkshakes with my double doubles at In-N-Out. Although I thought In-N-Out had mediocre burgers I found myself eating there every day because there was always a line of cars at the drive through windows. There was something about waiting to get a burger that made it worthwhile.

On Wednesday morning at nine o'clock I drove to Hollywood Park for an appointment with Mike Stewart of the Marketing Department. I had given him no information other than I was interested in writing a screenplay about horse racing. Stewart was a young, block headed jock who looked a couple of years removed from playing linebacker for the Miami Hurricanes.

"How are you, Mr. Rubin," he said with tremendous and what I assumed was phony concern.

"Good, Mr. Stewart," I said, hoping my hand wasn't broken from his power shake.

"Take a seat, buddy." He pointed to a single chair in front of a clutter free desk. A huge photo of Secretariat winning the Belmont Stakes by thirty-one lengths was on the wall in back of him.

"What can I do for you, Sid?"

"I'm a screenwriter based in New York City. I'm working on a story about horse racing. I'd love to gain access to the backstretch, observe the sights and sounds, talk to the trainers, grooms, and owners. It would be invaluable."

"Why not do this in New York, Sid? You're a long way from home."

"With winter coming my agent thought I'd get more work done out west. After all, even with the winterized track at Aqueduct there are lots of days lost to inclement weather."

"Not to mention freezing your writerly balls off." He said this without a hint of rancor. Mike might actually be a nice guy, although I wouldn't want to reach for a high pass in his part of the zone.

"Have you written a movie I might have heard of?"

"I don't know," I said. "Have you seen *More Horrible Than Death*?" His mouth dropped in awe.

"You -- you wrote *More Horrible than Death*?"

"Co-wrote the script and the song over the credits, too."

A college buddy came up with the idea and enlisted my help in writing it. I made $3,000 and he made millions. *More Horrible than Death* was to exploitation movies what Adolf Hitler was to political statesmen. In it the most grisly forms of death are depicted. My particular favorite was of a garbage man falling into a dumpster and being compacted into a neat little brick with just a tuft of brown toupee sticking out of the top.

"Gosh, Sid, *More Horrible Than Death* is one of the great ones. How did you get that footage of the anaconda eating that Nigerian baby?" As I told him he started filling out forms. I signed a couple of copies and we chatted about everything from the weather to his new bride. When the paperwork was finished, Stewart snapped a Polaroid of me, went to a laminating machine, pressed a few buttons and out popped a card featuring yours truly and the word PRESS. I clipped it to my jacket lapel. I now had instant access to the backstretch at Hollywood Park.

"Great to meet you, Sid. If you need anything, let me know." Stewart stood up, grabbed my hand, and again pulverized it

"Thanks, Mike. You've been great."

"Hey, it's my job."

I was at the door when I heard him call.

"Hey, Sid."

I turned to face him.

"Yes, Mike?"

"Your last name. Rubin. You know, we had a jockey ride here at Hollywood who had the same last name."

"Yes, I've heard of him."

"You any relation, Sid? You any relation to John Rubin?"

CHAPTER TWENTY - TWO

I was tempted to test out my new press pass but felt too tired. I was sure Stewart could see through my story. My being in California seemed an abrogation of my spiritual path. I belonged with my loyal, lovely wife, living honestly, pursuing my writing, going to AA meetings and experiencing the joy of living.

I stopped at an In-N-Out on Sunset and ate my double-double while driving back to The Surf. On the way I ducked into a deli on Fairfax called Cantor's and bought a slab of seven-layer cake the size of my thigh. By the time I reached the motel I was properly narcotized. Mitra intercepted me as I staggered back to my room.

"Hello, Mr. Sid you have the chocolate on your mouth and face."

"Thank you, Mitra," I said as I ran my hand over the grease.

"Do you play the cards, Mr. Sid?"

"Cards?"

"Because I play gin and I need a partner."

"I have to lie down," I said.

"You're not looking so peachy," she nodded. "You have the bug or something?"

"I'll be okay," I said. "Just hold my calls for the next few hours."

"You never get any calls," she said.

"Whatever."

I got to the room and threw myself on the bed. A Clint Eastwood movie was on HBO. As I settled into a comfortable position I felt a slight urge to pee. Once this urge presents, no matter how slight, it cannot be ignored, unless one is in a drunk tank with one toilet and sixty desperados, which I have been, in which case it can.

As I got up to take a leak I passed the hooker ads on the dresser. I took them into the bathroom. An ad saying GREAT HEAD and body to match attracted my attention. The woman in the ad was cute, brunette, with full lips, and young. I took the ad back to bed. Why not call, why not experience a little bliss. $200? I couldn't spend an eighth of my stake on a hand job. I muted the Eastwood movie, got some lotion, and gave myself imaginary head. It was over quickly. My depression was mitigated somewhat by the thought that I had just saved $200. I stayed in bed waiting for darkness, waiting for hunger, waiting for truth.

Around six o'clock I wandered into the lobby to find Mitra playing solitaire at a bridge table. She was always in the office. I wondered if she lived there.

"Mr. Sid, how are you?"

"Tired and old, Mitra. Old and tired."

"Join the club. You play gin?"

"Sure."

"Penny a point, five cents a box, dollar a game, double for spades sound okay?"

"I don't gamble."

"You woke up today, didn't you?"

"I think so."

"Then you gamble! Come then, indulge an old woman a bit of excitement."

I thought, well, I bought my mom lottery tickets for her birthday and that's technically gambling. And how could I get hurt at a penny a point? It was time to stop being so strict, so unbending. It was time to enjoy life.

I pulled up a seat. We played for hours. Mrs. Singh was a

good player, although after a few hands I knew exactly where she was keeping her high and low melds. Also, she was an inveterate "trailer", which meant she followed my discards with similar cards. Consequently I fished her for lots of useful tickets.

Our game was interrupted by an occasional check in. Mitra was good with the guests. Every once in a while a buxom young beauty swept by, giving Mitra a hug and grabbing a key from a plaque behind the desk. I assumed these girls were helping some of the male guests to "think clearly".

We quit just before midnight as we both wanted to watch "Die Hard" on HBO. I was ahead $31. Mitra wanted to settle up but I declined, saying we'd run a tab. She hugged me as I left, thanking me for the best time ever in her entire motel life. As I was walking out the door I, said, "Hey Mitra. Before I came out here I'd been getting postcards from The Surf. Do you know anything about that?"

"Postcards?" she said. "I don't think so, Mr. Sid."

I nodded. Then I thought: My God. I'm a betting man again.

CHAPTER TWENTY - THREE

After a couple of days playing gin and lying on my bed watching HBO I was paralyzed by indecision. My sleuth-like instincts were mordant.

I roused myself and went forth. If I didn't I'd soon own the motel, as I was up $263 on Mitra. She wasn't a bad gin player but she pressed, which meant she got uptight when she lost. There's not a good card in the world or a winning bet that will grace a pressing bettor. The only way to win is to relax, accept the bounty, kiss it, and caress it.

I found my hand meandering to my crotch. I missed Debra. I missed putting my finger in her ass when I fucked her. I missed taking my cock out of her cunt at the moment of orgasm and putting it in her mouth and shooting, shooting, spurting warm cream down her gullet and lying there afterwards, spent, afraid to let her go. For if I did would she still be there or be a figment of my imagination?

I drove down to Hollywood Park. The stable area at the track had just one vehicular entrance, on a service road a few blocks east of Prairie Avenue. It extended north about a half mile before it hooked west. About fifty yards up was an imposing security booth that required identification before being granted entry. Four large video cameras were aimed at the gate. The gate could only be opened by a guard inside the booth.

My press badge worked like a charm. Before the gate opened a security guard checked the bottom of my car with a mirror and had me sign a roster with my name and time of visit. He handed me a little plastic diagram of the stable area and pointed out a visitor's parking lot. I parked and walked across a small lawn and, presto, I was in the stable area.

Each barn contained twenty stalls. Various stables might share the same barn. Smaller stables got fewer stalls. Stall numbers proceeded sequentially from one to eight hundred. There were eight hundred stalls contained within forty barns.

The name of each stable was indicated by a plaque over the first stall it occupied. In some cases great artwork embellished the ownership. For instance, Peachtree Stable was denoted by a flowering peach tree painted in bright watercolor on the stable wall. Golden Eagle Farm featured a fierce, wing-stretched eagle over its plaque.

I took my time strolling along a dirt path which ran outside the stalls, aware of the sights, sound and smells. I had to jump off the path to avoid the occasional hot walker leading a horse. Most of the horses had just returned from workouts and walked with heads bowed, exhibiting none of the high- spiritedness one associated with thoroughbreds. Most barns were clean. Cinches, bridles, halters, saddles, brushes of many kinds and a host of gardening-type equipment hung neatly from hooks on the wooden walls. Bales of hay and alfalfa were stored neatly in the corner of each stall or outside. Most horses stood with their heads out of the stalls, some tethered to a ring on the stable door or wall. One out of maybe ten lied on its side sleeping, sides heaving slowly and deeply with each breath. An occasional goat, cat or dog meandered down the path or was inside the stall with the horse. Horses were known to enjoy the company of small animals and I have heard tales of insane horses who became tractable and successful after a pet was provided as a companion.

Most of the grooms were black or Spanish and seemed to have little on their minds other than tending to their charges. No one paid me any heed.

The stable map revealed the Robert Lemmons horses were in Barn Six. He had the first eleven stalls. Barn Six was on the westernmost portion of the complex. I glanced up at the sky, noted the position of the sun, and moved away from it. Within a couple of minutes I arrived at Barn Six.

It was eerily quiet. Horse heads stuck out of all eleven stalls. They made not a sound and if there were any other humans or pets around they weren't stirring. I walked slowly down the row of horses, looking at laminated 3x5 index cards placed in brass brackets beneath each stall door. Here was Good Time Day, a three year old bay gelding. Then Harriet Jones, a two year old chestnut filly, and so on. Lemmons's stable was clean. There wasn't a straw out of place.

"Hello," I called out. "Hello." A horse in a far off stall whinnied. Still no trace of humans. I backtracked to the front of the stable and spotted a small building set ten yards back. A gold banner held by string tied to a fence behind proclaimed BOB LEMMONS BARN – HOME OF CHAMPIONS. I went up three steps, opened a screen door, and knocked on a sturdy wooden one. A bird chirped in the distance. I knocked again. I placed my hand on the doorknob and turned gently.

The door swung open without resistance.

CHAPTER TWENTY - FOUR

It was a small office containing a desk, two chairs, file cabinet and several horse photos on the walls. I took the seat in front of the desk and waited. I didn't move a muscle for five minutes. I then got up and peered through the screen door. No sign of movement.

I moved behind the desk. A narrow drawer under the desktop was locked. A row of three larger drawers descended down the left side. The first drawer opened to reveal files. In a narrow space in front was a gun. Using a Starbuck's napkin, I gently lifted it. It looked like a snub nose .38 and it was loaded. I gently placed it back in the drawer in the exact place I found it.

The second drawer contained plaques and a few small trophies. One gold-plated trophy said 1975 TURF PARADISE TRAINER OF THE YEAR. Turf Paradise was a small, cheap track outside Phoenix. Another prize was a glass ball attached to a slab of wrought iron upon which was scripted 1981 KINDERGARTEN STAKES, PIMLICO RACE TRACK and underneath: Vintage Pride, Parsley Stables, Trainer Robert Lemmons.

There were several more awards but nothing more recent than 1981. Apparently Lemmons was not the kind of guy who liked to display his achievements. Or maybe when there weren't any more successes he decided not to advertise his fall from grace.

The bottom drawer contained office supplies – pens, legal

pads, rubber bands, staplers. I returned to the file drawer. I was about to pull it open when I heard a crunching sound outside. I slammed the drawer onto my left thumb. The pain was unbelievable. For a second I felt as if I would faint. I staggered to the chair and threw myself into it. I checked the thumb. A long, ragged gash extended about an inch above the nail. For a second I thought it was okay. Then blood started spurting, keeping perfect time with my rapid heartbeat. I plunged it into my mouth. If Lemmons walked in he would discover a 41 year old man sucking his thumb.

But no one entered. I rushed to the door and peered through the screen. Yards away a small squirrel danced about in a small pile of leaves, foraging for food. That was it.

I walked back to the stables. Still not a soul. I took my thumb out of my mouth. The bleeding had abated. I hoped I didn't need stitches. More important, I hoped I could deal gin hands to Mitra.

I returned to the office, wrapped the Starbuck's napkin around the wound. I examined the files. The first contained pink, alphabetized ownership papers. I quickly flipped to "P", found a document for Princess Bride, folded it, and placed it in my back pocket. The next file contained feed bills records, employment records, workout results, yearling purchases, shipping bills, and veterinarian reports. All extended back to 1970. It wasn't for lack of organization that Lemmons had fallen on hard times.

I went back to the desktop drawer. It had a lock into which a small key would fit. I took my penknife and twisted a couple of times. I yanked on it and smacked my injured thumb on the top ledge of the desk. I nearly screamed as the bloody Starbucks napkin and injured thumbnail lifted off and flew into the air. I got on my hands and knees trying to find the nail. After a while I found it. I thrust it in my jacket pocket wondering if it could be reattached. I stuck the tattered napkin back onto what was left of my thumb.

I banged on the desk remembering to use my good hand. The desktop drawer sprung out and slammed into my nuts. The pain exceeded the thumb injury. When I regained my senses I rummaged through the drawer like a maniac, knowing that if I was caught the least of my worries would be a lost fingernail. There was nothing of interest, merely a mélange of receipts, rubber stamps, bank deposit slips and bankbooks. As I was about to shut the drawer I saw, peeking out from the back, a wallet-sized blue notebook. I took it out and opened it.

As I read, the hairs on the back of my neck straightened, curled, and straightened again. Someone had written on the first page "Unexplained Disappearances, Suggested Motivations and Unusual Methods of Execution".

As I flipped through I encountered newspaper and computer-generated articles on boats lost in the Bermuda Triangle, caravans vanishing in the Gobi, disappearing airliners, and so on. There were articles on alien abductions, dematerialization rays, time machines, and particle regeneration. It was a book of madness and complicity, tomfoolery and skullduggery.

I just finished reading when I heard footsteps coming across the yard. I threw the book back into the drawer, slammed it, and hurled myself into the chair. No one came in. I went to the screen door. The yard was empty.

I ran, making a beeline for my car and safety.

CHAPTER TWENTY - FIVE

I spent the afternoon at the track watching the races. During each race as the horses pounded down the backstretch I tried to imagine how a horse could vanish. As I left the track I glanced at the guy selling the next day's Racing Forms. I was tempted to buy one for reference purposes but decided against it.

My Band Aid swathed thumb held up nicely during a few games of gin the next morning.

"You're beating me up, Sidney," said Mitra. I had just double-schneided her, putting me $363 to the good. I was wondering if she was going to pay or apply the total against the motel tab.

"I cannot get a card," she continued. "I am always losing. So then, Sidney, I ask you, if I am the one always to lose, why is it that you always appear to have lost?"

"What do you mean?"

"What a sour expression you have on your face! Day or night, whenever I see you it appears you just received the bad news. Why is that so?"

"I'm sorry. I'm actually overjoyed. It's just my way of showing it."

"Funny boy. If you don't want to talk to me, that's one thing. But don't lie to an old woman. And, if you think about it, a friend."

I thought, why not.

I told her about my brother. My gambling and drinking history. Loving Debra. Leaving Debra. The whole deal. She said not a word. Sat there with her eyes half-closed, taking in my story. After what seemed like forever I ran out of words and picked up the deck. Before I could deal she spoke.

"Thank you Sidney for the confidence. No, don't deal the cards quite yet. I want to have a word with you."

"Sure thing. I've been doing all the talking anyway."

"The problem," she said, "or the reason that you always appear to be in disharmony is that you are in disharmony. Nothing you do is good enough for you. Being with your wife, not enough. Finding your brother, not enough. Making a bet, not enough. Not making a bet, not enough. All your actions are contradicting one another. Why is that Sidney? Why is everything not enough?"

Part of me was thinking: hey let's play gin. Another part was thinking: who is this spiritual mama? Of course, neither one of these thoughts was enough.

"I don't know, Mitra. You tell me."

"I will tell you. I see it all the time, for many years. I see it in the men who stay at The Surf. Family men, many of them, and yet, during their stay, they obtain the services of one of my girls. They are thrilled always."

"The girls are exciting and clean, right?"

"Squeaky. So these men enjoy the experience and then, later, when I see them, they appear miserable and ridden with the guilt. Like you, for them nothing is enough. Nothing is morally correct."

"Isn't that to be expected from someone who has just cheated on his wife?"

"There is no such thing as guilt. There is only following one's nature. And more importantly, accepting it. You struggle, struggle with the excitement of the races versus the ordinary part of life represented by your wife. You think you love her which complicates the struggle. You crave the horse handicapping, a lonely path, and yet it is your soul. But your feeling for Debra lures you in the direction of service to another human being. What does one do?"

I wanted to scream "What, okay, what?" but I was silent. She took the deck from me and shuffled. I waited for her to continue but she didn't. She rallied nicely in the last game and hit me for $23. On the way out of the office she hugged me.

"Don't worry so much, Sidney. Think about what I tell you. Acknowledge your nature. Do not fear it. Only you can decide what it is. But decide now, this minute. Let your need take you where it will. Every life is sacred and every life informs the rest. We learn from all spirits. What appears to be an errant path is illuminating and wondrous in its own right." She kissed my cheek. I was embarrassed to feel a stirring in my loins.

When I got back to my room there was a large gift basket by my door piled high with cheeses, dried meats, crackers, and chocolates. A little card perched at the top read, "Thinking of You". It was signed "A Secret Admirer". I picked it up and carried it into my room.

I had no idea who this was from but I was all for gift baskets. I had actually sent one to myself one lonely Christmas. I grabbed a pepperoni stick and went out to get a bite to eat. There was a scraggly homeless guy sitting by my car. He was holding a large sign that said COME TO CRAVEDORE. I gave him the pepperoni stick and drove away.

I feasted on two chicken pot pies and three biscuits at a KFC on La Cienega. When I pulled back into The Surf parking lot I was tired. I needed to sleep. When I woke up maybe some of this would make sense.

I pulled into my spot. I saw the homeless man to whom I had given the pepperoni. He was lying on his back, staring sightlessly into space. It looked like he was dead.

A half eaten pepperoni stick was next to him.

CHAPTER TWENTY - SIX

Once inside the room the fear hit. It grabbed my nut sack and squeezed until I felt as if I was getting the world's longest hernia exam. I wanted to get into my little Neon and flee this addled city, drive north, maybe. I heard Seattle was nice. Or maybe back to Debra. It was suddenly a comforting thought, spending the rest of my days writing useless screenplays and working as a stock clerk in an air-conditioning store.

I called Debra. By a miracle she answered on the fourth ring.

"Debra, it's Sid. Please don't hang up."

"Sid, do you know what time it is?"

"About midnight."

"That's three o'clock New York time."

"Honey, I'm sorry. It's an emergency." There was a pause.

"What's wrong?"

"It's that, I think someone killed this homeless man. I think they meant to kill me."

"Sid, are you drinking again?"

"No, but it's beginning to seem like a viable option."

"You have the same wild tone. Like you've had a few."

"Debra, please believe me. I've seen a lot of strange things. I can't make sense of it. I'm in a little room at a cheap motel and I have no reality."

"It's pills, isn't it."

"No. I swear I'm sober."

"Sid, do you want to come home?"

She didn't waste time. She cut right to the center, to my fear and courage, approach and avoidance, the heart of my ambivalence.

"I don't know," I said.

"Wrong answer, Sid."

I heard the click and it was like snapping a string off my life vest, sending me tumbling helplessly into a churning sea. I dragged the desk to the door and wedged it under the doorknob. I went to the bathroom and as I took a leak I idly stropped my penknife against the brick wall.

You know this fear, I thought. It was the same as losing a big bet in the 7th at Aqueduct and having just enough money left to pay the rent. But you like a horse in the last race. The thought of risking the rent money on that horse produces this same fear…and intoxication. It is all the money you have and money is life. There is no life without money. There is no money without love.

This was the moment of truth. The moment when the match of fear would ignite a conflagration of cowardice or be doused by the ice water in my veins. I poked the tip of my left index finger with the penknife. A small dot of blood appeared.

I pulled the desk away from the door and walked out into the parking lot. Death at that moment meant nothing other than the absence of want and at that moment I wanted nothing. Fear flew from me like a jilted lover.

Of course, the bum and his sign were gone. It's the way everything was out in Los Angeles. There wasn't any gravity and people and things just pulled free from their moorings and vanished.

I got in my trusty Neon and drove north on La Cienega to a place called Norm's and drank coffee until shards of orange light knifed through a navy blue night sky.

I tipped the waiter $5, and got into my car, and drove to Hollywood Park to see Mr. Robert Lemmons.

CHAPTER TWENTY - SEVEN

Lemmons was in a stall running his hand down a horse's legs when I arrived. I was surprised to hear him speaking fluent Spanish to a groom. Lemmons noticed me almost immediately.

"Can I help you?" he asked.

"I'm Sid Rubin, John Rubin's older brother."

"Why hello," said Lemmons. He was short but his hand enveloped mine with a calloused strength. "Good to see you."

"Fuck you, Lemmons."

"Say again?"

"Fuck you and the horse you rode in on."

"You have a strange way of getting to know folks," he said. "Talking that way may not be such a good idea."

"Fuck you," I said. I fingered the penknife in my pocket.

"You don't know who I am," Lemmons said. "In fact, you don't know me at all."

"I know you're a crooked trainer and you're involved with my brother's disappearance."

"In honor of John I'll pretend I didn't hear that. So I won't strangle you."

"I'd like to see you try."

"Nah, you wouldn't."

"What was it, Lemmons? An insurance scam?"

Lemmons sighed and shook his head.

"Insurance? Princess Bride wasn't worth her feed bills. She was a sweet filly but if she stayed healthy and raced until she was six or seven I doubt she'd be anything more than a barn pet."

"Then what?"

"First, you owe me an apology."

"Okay. I'm sorry I talked that way."

"That's not what I mean."

I looked at him blankly

"Come up to the office and I'll show you. It's Sid, isn't it?"

"Yeah."

I trod the familiar ground to Lemmon's office. Once inside he opened the top left desk drawer. I tensed, certain he would come out with the gun. Instead, he held a small, security camera-type videocassette. I glanced up at the ceiling and spotted the small video camera dangling from wires in the left corner.

He popped the tape into a machine on the corner of the desk. In short order I saw myself losing a thumbnail and taking a desk drawer in the nuts, all in high def.

"You're a dangerous man," said Lemmons with a chuckle.

"I'm sorry I went through your things."

"I accept your apology. If it was my brother I'd feel the same way. I might go about things differently but who knows."

"What do you think happened to him?" I asked.

He shrugged. "I'm a horse trainer, not a detective."

"But the book on disappearances…"

"Ah, that. Look, I'm just trying to make sense of this along with everybody else. My niece is an Internet freak. She got me these half-baked articles and I stuck 'em in the blue book."

"I thought there was more to it."

"Sid, I'm an ordinary guy. Grew up in Nebraska, slept in a barn, been around horses all my life. I don't know nothin' bout nothin' except maybe, if a horse comes along that can run a lick, to get out of the way long enough to let him do it."

"You used to be more successful."

He sighed deeply. "Yep, the young studs have taken over

with their medicines, supplements, Arab owners, shady vets and newfangled training methods. I guess I haven't changed with the times. 'Course, maybe if I was a little more diplomatic with the owners it would help. But I'm sixty-two years old. At a certain point you are who you are."

"How well did you know my brother?

"Johnny and I were close. He broke bread a couple of Sundays with me and the Misses. He was a good boy."

"What did he tell you about me?"

Lemmons coughed and arranged papers on his desk.

"He said you had gambling problems. That betting the ponies caused you grief. Said if you came around to let him know."

"He thought I was nuts, huh."

"Oh no," said Lemmons. "Not at all. In fact, he said you were a horserace handicapping genius. That you had a gift."

I almost cried, I could have, a knot in my throat swelled until I could barely swallow. I felt it was bad form to blubber in front of a man I had told to fuck himself five minutes before. I calmed down and listened.

"Yeah," continued Lemmons, "John said you had gone through a lot of pain playing the horses. But that you got to a point where you knew what you were doing with a Racing Form. I heard you did good in some of those Vegas tournaments."

"I was starting to."

"You got to be sharp to do that. But you gave it all up. Why?"

"Booze got in the way."

"It's a problem for a lot of people," said Lemmons. "John was disappointed. He thought you could have made big money at it."

"I thought John felt I was a degenerate. His agent, Gustavo Clemente, told me if I bothered John he would kill me."

Lemmons leaned back in his chair and laced his fingers behind his head. He didn't say a word for a couple of minutes.

"Your brother had a great future, Sid. He was a good little rider and he was a sponge. I never saw him make the same mistake twice. Gustavo Clemente was the right man for John at the time.

Taking John to Panama to learn to ride was a lucky break. But it was getting to the point where Clemente was gonna have to go."

"Why?"

"Because he's dangerous. In his own mind, anyway."

"What do you mean?"

"He tried to control John. Who he spoke to, where he went, what he did. If another jockey agent so much as said hello to John, Clemente would go nuts. Gustavo wasn't about to take a chance on losing his meal ticket."

"My brother was that good?"

"He was getting to be. It didn't hurt that he was Jewish. Out here in California a lot of Jewish folks are horse owners. They were drooling at the chance to hoist a Bar Mitzvah boy onto one of their derby hopefuls."

"I gotta ask again. This Clemente. Is he really dangerous?"

"Most guys, when they talk they're not dangerous. The louder and longer they yak, the less apt they are to do something stupid.. Clemente was a talker. But I saw him pop a couple of guys in the middle of a sentence. Only a wack job'll do that."

"If I came out here after Clemente warned me not to, do you think he'd do something?"

Lemmons grinned. "Hell yeah, Sid, and it wouldn't be pretty. You eaten yet?"

"Nah, just ten cups of coffee at Norm's on La Cienega."

"Come with me while I take a spin around the barn. Then I'll buy you breakfast at our backstretch four-star restaurant. We'll have us a nice plateful of grub and discuss something near and dear to our hearts."

"What's that?"

"Horses, Sid. And horse race handicapping."

CHAPTER TWENTY - EIGHT

After I left Lemmons I was depressed. He kept trying to convince me to handicap horses. To follow my true nature. He sounded like Mitra. The more he talked the more tired I became.

There was nothing I wanted to do, nothing I could do. I was not a husband. I was not a writer, not a musician. I was not a woman. I was not a Shiite Muslim. I was not an observant Jew. I had forgotten my Jewish roots. The God Of The Jews would not let me wander so miserably in this emotional desert, would he?

It occurred that this was a test powered by fear and need for some greater purpose. I hoped that it became clear before long.
I didn't want to handicap, participate in a marriage, work, write, do much of anything. The thought came to end it all. It was amazing how thoughts flit through our minds like small birds. Fortunately, they keep whizzing about and rarely alight, for if they did…

I returned to The Surf to find Mitra sitting in a chair outside her office shuffling a deck of cards.

"I'm not feeling so good," I said.

"A game will pick you up, Sidney. Who can resist a shoe of gin with someone as charming as myself?"

She flashed her even white teeth. We headed into the office and played for a while. My depression lifted slightly although she won and trimmed the deficit to just over $400. I left at about one o'clock and grabbed a Double-Double at the In-N-Out on Sunset. I ducked into a bathroom in a Shell Station and counted my money: almost $1,400.

I drove east on Sunset watching the occasional elderly person or youngster shuffling along the boulevard. No one seemed to be middle-aged in California, just young or old. For some reason, I made a left on Cahuenga and headed north. As I approached Hollywood Boulevard I spotted a newsstand on the right and pulled into a five minute loading zone.

It was a well-stocked newsstand complete with every conceivable magazine and large paperback book section as well. On a tray near the cash register was a stack of Racing forms.

I thought of Mitra and Lemmons. I loved handicapping. It was my passion and my life. Forgive me Debra for I know not what I do. I gave the tattooed young clerk a fin and he handed me a copy of the next day's Racing Form.

Back at The Surf I opened the paper and read the articles. Jockeys were injured, suspended and/or successful. Slot machines were reviving flagging fortunes at various tracks. Several horses were touted as derby contenders. A pharmacist from New Jersey, a casual weekend player, won $115,000 in a contest at Bally's Hotel in Vegas. A dude like that, stepping in shit. What chance would he have against a genius like me?

I quickly turned to the past performances. The first at Hollywood had five entries, upscale fillies and mares running for a big purse. I tried to concentrate but made no sense of the data. Numbers remained numbers, nothing more. I plugged along for several minutes but it got worse. My eyelids came down as if attached to weights and I fell into a deep sleep. I awakened confused and frightened, the Racing Form on my chest.

I didn't remember buying it. I heaved it against the wall, pages flying in all directions. I got into the bathroom and splashed water on my face. The mirror revealed the face of a betrayer. This can't be happening. I had lost my way. O mother, where art thou, where were you ever? I need to sleep with you and hold you. I want to make love to you, mother.

I clutched the side of the sink trying to squeeze these insane thoughts out of my head. I was a horse-race handicapper. I was on a mission to find my brother. Things I knew: beer was good, two beers were great, three bears, ecstasy. I must get a beer and fuck one of Mitra's whores. I wanted to fuck her good, give her a goodbye fuck before I killed her. I wanted to paint the walls of my motel room crimson with her tainted blood. I wanted AIDS, to die wasting away in my excrement reading the Racing Form, known throughout the industry as a pillar of handicapping wisdom. I was not a derelict, I was a horserace handicapper. I figure out winning horses. I think outside the box. I am not an addict, Debra. If I was could I have contained myself for the past four years? No bets in four years, my little nurse provider. I wonder whose cock you're sucking now, my little cocksucker.

Fuck me and fuck the Surf and fuck food. I was lost. I picked up the Racing Form, put it back together and turned to the third race at Hollywood. Only six horses entered. An Argentinean import piqued my interest. I tried to focus on the race but my mind kept wandering.

CHAPTER TWENTY - NINE

"The truth is," Lemmon said, "you have no chance to find out what happened to John. No one does and the faster you come to grips with that the better off you'll be."

I had been sitting in my usual grandstand seat one afternoon watching the races when Lemmons joined me. It had been three days since our backstretch breakfast. Since then I had whiled my time away watching HBO, jacking off, wandering around LA and observing the races in the afternoons. I had not bought the Racing Form since my breakdown at the Surf. I thought God had sent me a message that day, informing me that if I started handicapping again bad things would happen.

"I don't know, Bob. Can I call you Bob? I'm trying not to think about it."

"What are you doing if not to find your brother? I don't see a Racing Form."

"I've been wondering the same thing. I think I have nowhere else to go."

He nodded. I didn't know if it was agreement or sympathy. We sat in silence. The field for the sixth pranced onto the track. It was a turf race featuring a full field of colts and geldings, bred in California, and which had not won two races other than maiden or claiming. At this level it was possible a horse could have talent. I glanced at the six horse in my program, who was named Dynaday, whose father was Dynaformer, a great grass sire. Since I didn't have The Form I didn't know what he had done. He was listed at 6-1 on the tote board so I figured he had shown a thing or two. As he cantered by he was focused and professional, ears pricked, mouth taking full hold of the bit without a trace of rankness. The jockey sat raised off the saddle, orange silks moving in perfect rhythm with his gait. I decided to watch Dynaday during the race.

"I missed you," said Lemmons. "Thought you'd come around."

"And do what? I bought the Racing Form. Could barely look at it. Made me crazy."

"Why?"

"I don't know. It was like there was something immoral about it. They say you can never go back."

"Depends to what."

"Maybe those goddamn Twelve Step meetings ruined it for me.They say the program works that way. You ask for God's will be done once too often and it may differ from your will."

"To handicap?"

"Yeah." Lemmons continued to sit next to me. I'm surprised he didn't leave.

Dynaday went off at 9-2. He took the lead and the fractions were legitimate. As he passed the part of the race where my brother disappeared. I strained to imagine Dynaday galloping into another dimension. I envisioned Dynaday's electrons separating and dispersing, flung into a random universe by an unseen hand. I was brought back to reality by race caller Long's voice. I watched Dynaday lengthen his stride and turn into the lane six lengths to the good. The jockey was looking over his shoulder for non-existent competition. Dynaday won under wraps and paid $12 to win.

"You were watching him, weren't you. Dynaday," said Lemmons.

"Yeah. But I don't have The Form. I had no idea what he was going to do."

"The hell," rejoined Lemmons. "Your intuition was talking

to you as loud as Long's race call."

"I liked the breeding and he looked great on the track. But you know as well as I do the racetrack is filled with well-bred suckers who can't outrun a fat man."

Lemmons whipped a Racing Form out of his back pocket and thrust it in front of me. I forced myself to look. This was Dynaway's fifth lifetime start. He won his last race on the turf after a no-try first race prep off a layoff. Both horses he beat in his last start came back to win. Strong.

"Imagine if you were handicapping the race," said Lemmons, "and then seen him on the track. I imagine it'd be chicken for dinner, wouldn't it, son."

"Who knows." This urging me to get back into the game was wearying. Yet I found myself mentally computing that a $100 win bet on Dynaway would have returned better than $600.

"Nothing wrong with making money, son," Lemmons said. "Especially if you don't know where your next buck is coming from."

I thought about how much fun handicapping had been. About how close I had come. About the gift my brother said I had.

I turned to speak to Lemmons. The seat was empty, as if I had imagined the whole thing.

CHAPTER THIRTY

Maybe it was a few nights later. I lost track of time. HBO was playing nonstop. Mitra let herself into my room. Apparently she had been knocking at my door and calling for several days. The light which blazed into the room as she opened the door blinded me.

"Mr. Sid, are you ill?" she asked, coming over and sitting on the bed.

She put her hand on my forehead. Smooth and cool. "No, you feel okay. I have brought you a chilled Yoo Hoo and several Nabisco shortbread cookies."

I was far from hungry but I let her lift my head and drizzle Yoo Hoo down my throat. Oddly, I didn't gag.

"Tell her about when we used to throw rocks at cans in the woods" said my brother. He was sitting in the chair by the dresser dressed, as usual, in cerise jockey silks.

"I never threw rocks with you," I replied. "I played with dad. You were too young and stupid. Nobody liked you."

"No, you loved me," said John. "It was natural for you to feel anger when I was born. You didn't have mom and dad all to yourself."

"I hated them too," I said. "Who wanted them for anything?"

"Aw Sid," he said.

"There, there," Mitra chimed in. She was stroking my

forehead, lying beside me, thin body pressed against mine.

"You mustn't worry," she said. "You merely want to find the truth of your existence." I looked back to the chair and John was gone.

"Is that what this is?" I asked her.

"And more," she replied. "Imagine if you will an impoverished village in India, mud huts, many people hungry and afflicted with unmentionable diseases, drought, insects, no life at all. And in all of this a sense of benevolence and gratitude. What do you make of that?"

"I don't know." She put one spindly leg across my abdomen. She was kissing my cheek. Her breath was rosemary and thyme and Yoo Hoo.

"It is not what we want, not what we have. It is what we are. In Cravedore."

"Where?"

"Cravedore, my village."

The name resonated. Cravedore. Where had I heard that name?

"How can one miss something which is so dispiriting? Yet I miss my birthplace and it is lost forever in my past."

"Cravedore."

"Yes. A mere one hundred and fifty kilometers south of Calcutta. Do you know, during the monsoon season, Cravedore is actually under water much--"

--and I remembered. The homeless man outside my hotel room. The guy who had died and disappeared. The guy with the cardboard sign which said COME TO CRAVEDORE.

I was dimly aware of Mitra's tongue making slow circles on my earlobe, her hand straying to my crotch.

"My goodness," she said. "You have the Member of Royalty. I should like to taste it."

I closed my eyes. If I fell into a deep sleep I would not be in a seedy motel room with a sixty year old Indian woman about to give me head. If I slept I would be where truth was tangible and compassion real.

My underpants were pulled down and Mitra's warm mouth was on me and I was helpless.

CHAPTER THIRTY - ONE

The following morning I made an effort. Shaved. Showered. Found fresh clothes. Outside it was warm for a November day. Wind gusts whipped fast food wrappers into yellow and orange tornados across the parking lot. I took the long way to the Neon so as to avoid Mitra's office.

I drove east on Beverly to the King's Road Café and grabbed a cup of diesel fuel they called coffee. I sipped and checked out the comely actresses in workout gear, icy women who sipped coffee and read the LA Times and Variety and blabbed into iPhones. I assumed they were actresses because they had nowhere to go. Like me.

I ducked into a bathroom and counted my money. About a thousand bucks. I guess you don't spend much when you lie in bed for days doing nothing but watching HBO.

I headed west on Beverly, took Wilshire into Santa Monica and headed north on Pacific Coast Highway. North of Temescal I pulled over, jaywalked across what was essentially a freeway, hopped a short wooden fence, and clambered down jagged rocks to a pristine beach. It must have been eighty-five degrees and gorgeous.

I arrived at the foot of the ocean, foam waves lapping at my feet. The water was green with algae. I pulled my shoes and socks off and waded in up to my ankles. I raised my arms over my head and remained there for a long time, asking for God's will to be done. There was no booming voice, flash of light, or burning bush. It occurred to me that I had forgotten sunscreen and jaywalked back to the car.

Continuing north I stopped at a restaurant called The Charthouse and got a delicious blackened fish sandwich. As I ate I felt lonelier than I ever had in my whole life.

On my way back to The Surf I picked up the Racing Form at a liquor store on Twenty-Sixth and Wilshire. I also purchased a Macanudo Hampton Court cigar. The tobacco was rich and nurturing. I drove and puffed, glancing at the Racing Form in the passenger seat. I didn't feel so lonely anymore.

CHAPTER THIRTY - TWO

I arrived at Hollywood Park just after the running of the third race. I took my seat in the grandstand and, as usual, I was the only one in the section.

I opened The Racing Form to the fourth race, creased the paper back and folded it. On the face of it the race was impenetrable, a six furlong maiden special weight affair. Many of the ten horses entered had never even started. The only information to be gleaned was a string of workouts listed beneath the horse's name. I did not trust workouts as they usually took place early in the morning away from public scrutiny. It would have been nice to believe clockers and trainers honestly reported workout times but why, in fact, would they do such a thing? The more hidden the information, the bigger the payoffs. Racetrackers understood this. Larceny was their currency.

I turned the page to the fifth. A race to be conducted at a mile and a sixteenth on the turf for horses which had never won a race other than maiden or claiming. Ten horses entered. Four or five speed horses that had raced near or on the lead. The rest lumbering types. Limited winners. Limited talent.

Something drew me to this race. I held the paper as if it was an extension of my arm. I felt power and confidence. A gull swooped by cawing appreciation. I stretched, got up and at a nearby concession stand bought a large cup of coffee. Splashed in a little cream substitute and returned to my seat.

I sipped and dissected the race. All playable races have a key which, when found, opens the door to riches. Without the key one may place a wager and get lucky and win. More often than not one will bounce off the door, bruised and broken.

I went over past performances again and again. I scanned back through each horse's races to see which speed horse, many months before, had shown the quickness it had been evincing in recent longer turf races. A tingle ran up the back of my neck as I realized none of the horses that had been flashing speed recently had shown that quality in faster, shorter races earlier in its career. It was possible each horse had improved dramatically or altered its running style successfully. It was more likely that they had been running against slower horses recently and only appeared to be running fast. There was the illusion of speed and nothing more.

Except one horse. A gelding named Hold the Mayo. His earlier races were peppered with sharp efforts against speedy sprinters who had subsequently won. Sometime in June the wheels began to come off and Hold The Mayo's connections dropped him in for a cheap claiming price. No one took the bait. The horse was then given a needed rest. He returned about a month ago and ran an even race in a relatively cheap sprint. He was then dropped to an even lower claiming level at a mile and wired the opposition in fast time. Off that race Hold the Mayo was claimed, or purchased, and was being triple jumped in value and entered on the different racing surface, the grass, for the first time. The new connections had high winning percentages and were apparently sharp and devious and Hold The Mayo had turf breeding in his pedigree.

The key to the race. I had found it. Hold The Mayo was the only legitimate speed horse. He was faster than the other horses. He was in good form. He was in the hands of a capable trainer. He had the illusion of not being good enough because of his recent cheap claiming price.

I flipped through the pages of the program to the 5th race.

The morning line listed Hold the Mayo at 20-1.

CHAPTER THIRTY - THREE

The odds for the fifth race blinked on the infield tote board and Hold The Mayo was thirty-five to one. I felt as if I had died and gone to horseplayer heaven. I delved more deeply into The Racing Form. Hold The Mayo looked better with each pass.

They paid almost one hundred grand for him at a sale in Keeneland as a two year old so I knew at one time he was thought to have ability. He was a Kentucky bred and they generally did not breed meatloaf in the Bluegrass State.

The interior fractions of his races stood up nicely. In his most recent win, albeit against slouches up north, he got the half in .46 and flashed six panels in 1:10.2. He was ready, no doubt.

With fifteen minutes to post, I did a little mediation. I watched with amusement as negative thoughts raced across my mind-sky like banners trailing from a message plane. "You're wasting your time," read one. "What are you doing here, Debra misses you," flashed another. "You degenerate scumbag, is this what it's come to?" went whipping by. It was amazing what presented when I was ready to take a chance.

I was aware of a presence next to me. It might have been my punishing superego but my punishing superego did not smell like Aqua Velva. I opened my eyes to see a swarthy, thin, mustachioed man rubbing shoulders with me. I glanced around to be certain several thousand fans had not poured into the grandstand during the two minutes I had been meditating. Nope. The only two seats taken were mine and his.

I made no move to get away. I could not will my legs to carry me from my birdshit-stained seat. I glanced at the fellow. He was staring at the infield as if he was the captain of a vessel heading for points unknown and the horizon was his only friend.

With eleven minutes to post time and Hold the Mayo drifting up to 40-1 he broke the silence.

You know, when I come to the USA from my native Panama I think it is the land of opportunity. Get rich quick thoughts dance in my head like pretty women. Now I am not so sure." I nodded my head in agreement as if I was from Central America.

"I lose my way but then I get lucky. I find a jockey so rare it is like being in a mango grove and discovering a clam with a pearl in it the size of a big rock." I realized the guy was Gustavo Clemente, my brother's agent, the guy who had threatened me and enjoyed cold-cocking folks during a casual conversation. C'mon, legs, I implored. But they were taking a siesta.

"I never seen nothing like it. Most of the time the kid is ordinary, no spark, no passion. But when he sits on a horse, mercy, he is riding in another, how do you say, dimencion? Being a jockey is everything to him. He rides each race as if it is his last."

The horses for the fifth were on the track. Hold The Mayo looked so good I wanted to cry. He bounced along with a coiled energy. The jockey stroked his neck, played with braids that had been carefully woven into his chestnut mane by a caring groom.

"Then one day, just like that, he is gone," continued Clemente. "He rides in a race, a race of no importance and disappears. I know the theories and silliness. Por dios, I am a suspect! They take me in and don't read me my rights and interrogate me for two days. After eight baloney sandwiches they let me out. I think about John, yes. I think about the force that drives him and his need to ride, ride, ride and he does, like, well, like he has to prove something. Who do you think he has to prove himself to, amigo?"

For an instant I thought the soliloquy was over.

"I tell you this, por seguro," Clemente continued abruptly. "I don't know what happens in that race. But I know why. *And why is what has brought you to this place. It is to fulfill the destiny of your brother.*"

Without another word he got up and walked away. I remained seated, staring at his seat, bathed in the lingering aftermath of his cheap aftershave. I glanced back at the track. Eight minutes to post. Hold the Mayo was taking some action. He was down to 24-1.

There is a moment when one is about to place a bet on a longshot, a horse only you believe in, when one has to trust. One has to trust that this thing, this illusion to which one is drawn and which no one else sees, is real. When a horse is in the 20-1 range and higher, in the absence of public support one must depend on an inner strength to summon the energy to make the bet.

I couldn't find this. I blamed it on Clemente's visit. I was a piker, a fool. My brother, the passionate one, was gone. My search for him had led me to the racetrack, the site of my undoing, and here I was attempting to raise his corpse by becoming one myself. All that was missing was a Budweiser in my hand.

Three minutes to post. I didn't move, I was not sure I could. Hold The Mayo drifted back to 30-1. A hundred bucks to win would return better than three thousand dollars. With a Herculean effort I got to my feet and wobbled into the grandstand. My right hand was inside my pocket holding my cash like a lifeline.

Two minutes. Hold The Mayo was up to 35-1. I walked up to a betting window. There were four guys in front of me, all with grey hair and none taller than five feet. Maybe the Home For Retired Jockeys was having a day at the races. Since I hadn't purchased a voucher I had to wait for a live teller to take my bet.

My fear took a different form. I was afraid I'd get shut out. One minute till post. Three guys were still in front of me.

"The horses are approaching the gate," intoned track announcer Long.

One guy got his tickets. Two guys in front of me. Maybe they were demented. Maybe they couldn't remember which horse they liked. I had no shot. I couldn't stand it, I needed to bet, I needed to be alright, Hold The Mayo was my ticket out of here but where was there?

"The horses are going into the gate."

The remaining guy in front of me was asking for combinations like he was at a Chinese restaurant. He finally moved away.

"They're in the gate." I lurched forward.

"A hundred to win on the seven," I croaked. I slid a Franklin across the counter. The teller pressed a couple of buttons. A ticket flew out of the machine's narrow aperture. He handed it to me. I grabbed it and studied it. Yes.

"Good luck," he said. I nodded. Luck has nothing to do with this, I thought, heading back to my section.

CHAPTER THIRTY - FOUR

I got a jolt when Hold the Mayo broke tardily for I expected him to take the lead. The jock gathered him in and took back in fifth or sixth place. Muscles tightened in my upper abdomen. As the field sailed around the first turn the talentless speed horses duked it out in slow factions.

Hold The Mayo cantered along. Going down the backstretch he maintained contact with the leaders without being asked although, without binoculars, it was hard to see if he was on the bit. As they approached the far turn the field was bunching and Hold the Mayo appeared to be bottled up. My mouth was so dry I could barely swallow. As they whipped into the stretch hold The Mayo was a scant three lengths from the leaders but had saved all the ground. The jock was riding as if he was in a stakes race - - and then he did a great thing. He eased Hold The Mayo off the fence for clear sailing. With a flick of his wrists and a left-handed tap of the whip on his shoulder, Hold the Mayo surged past the leaders and opened up by a length and a half. That was easy, maybe too easy. A sixteenth of a mile to payday.

The jock went to a left-handed whip. This was uncharted territory, Hold The Mayo had never run this far and never on the grass. C'mon baby. The race was in slow motion, everything was taking so damn long, the lead still a length and a half. Come on, baby, reach out Hold The Mayo and now the name sounded faintly ridiculous.

A hundred yards left to run, the lead was a length. My jockey switched the whip to his right hand, the strong hand, and I could hear the rat a tat of crop on horse flank. Eighty yards, a length lead, another jockey was pushing and scrubbing a horse on the outside, a blur of green silks, about a half length behind. Hold The Mayo stretched out, red eyes burning, c'mon baby you're BETTER than these horses, I know you are, I saw it in The Form, twenty yards, then, the other horse drove on the outside, five yards, and they FLASHED across the finish line together, Hold The Mayo and the green-silked number five horse.

I grabbed the Racing Form and looked to check out number five. Ah yes, a European import, a horse I categorized as one of the lumbering ones, sure, but he had never raced in this country and although those races were conducted at lesser European venues and at longer distances you could never discount a first time European on the turf and what was I thinking?

The photo took better than ten minutes. I sat in my seat watching Hold The Mayo and the European import make slow circles on the track by the finish line. The anxious owners of both horses milled nervously outside the winners circle. Finally, the photo sign went down. Numbers flashed on the tote board: 5-7-6. Hold The Mayo had been beaten. Within seconds the results were posted. The European import paid $21. Hold The Mayo paid $40 to place and $18 to show. My win ticket was useless. I took it out and stared at it. This piece of paper was a fraction of an inch away from being worth almost $4,000.

I made a feeble effort to handicap the next race and didn't have the energy. I felt as if I had personally run the last race, not the horse. He did everything but win. He ran a gallant race. As I walked out of the track I was reminded that this was a tough game and felt curiously optimistic.

CHAPTER THIRTY - FIVE

I found myself in a diner on Sunset eating French toast with a spoon. I asked for a fork several times and was ignored. They could smell the loss, I thought. Speaking of the loss, no matter how much syrup I slathered onto the barely soaked slices of Wonder Bread, the coma I so richly sought and deserved eluded me. My joy at my ability to pick a 35-1 contender had been replaced by a sodden sense of depression over getting nosed out of a four grand payday. It would be nice to have five g's in my pocket instead of just under a grand.

I finished, left the inept waitress a too-large five buck tip since I had nothing smaller and couldn't waste the time getting change. Which was funny, because my appointment book was not exactly teeming.

I walked to the Neon, uncertain where to go. I drove back to The Surf and walked into Mitra's office.

"I'll be checking out tomorrow," I said. She looked surprised.

"Why, Sidney? It is the experience we had the other evening?"

"Time to move on."

"But your work here isn't finished."

"What work?"

"Whatever drew you to The Surf in the first place," she said.

"You know, the surf is the first thing we see when we stand on the shore. It is but a small glimpse of the ocean itself.

To experience the truth of the water one must venture into it."

"Yeah, like I said, I'll be leaving The Surf."

"It is what happened the other night," she said. I saw before me a fragile, hungry woman who could devour me.

"Let me tell you something," she said. "Tonight I will treat you to a sacred experience with one of the girls. It's what you need."

"I can't afford it."

"Have you lost your hearing? It's my treat. I'll have Ricki come visit you in an hour. Why don't you go inside, have a hot shower, shampoo - - you do have shampoo, yes? - - lie down and watch some television. Ricki will be with you before you know it."

"Ricki."

"She is a trained masseuse, the best. I saw the certificates. Her hands melt men's minds."

"I don't know," I mumbled.

"On the house, Sidney. Don't be a fool. Pleasure is the highway, take it, speed on it, your nature beckons. Fly along and you may yet descend to your greatness."

"What – what did you say?"

She was on the phone, punching in numbers. "Ricki, it is Mitra. I have a darling for you. His emotions are bound up in his musculature, he cannot think clearly. He needs the premium package. Yes. Yes. In one hour, good, most definitely." She looked up.

"It is done, my New York amigo. Go along now. I need to watch the awards show on the Black TV Network."

I thanked her and headed out the door. I did exactly as she said. Showered and shaved for the second time that day. Lay down on the bed and watched TV. The Lakers were playing the Grizzles and Kobe Bryant was an acrobat. I closed my eyes for what seemed an instant and was awakened by a knocking on the door.

CHAPTER THIRTY - SIX

Mitra knew her girls. Ricki was a blonde fox in her twenties. She pummeled me like I was pizza dough. I was on my stomach and she was straddling me. With each press of her elbow into my back I emitted an involuntary grunt. We were naked.

"You like this?" she asked. She wasn't even out of breath. For some reason, I was.

"Yeah."

"How much?"

"I'm supposed to ask you how much."

She pressed an elbow deep into the right side of my back, a couple of seconds longer than necessary.

"Whoa, Nelly."

"You're a funny man, aren't you."

"Not really."

"Mitra tells me you're a horseplayer."

"I don't know what I am."

"You know all about the races, don't you, funnyman." I would have shrugged but my back was immobilized.

"I've been doing it for a long time."

"What's your favorite kind of race to play?"

"A race that makes sense."

"How do you know when a race makes sense?"

"I don't know until it does."

"But you might spend a lot of time handicapping a race and it might never make sense."

My mind idly wondered how she knew the word handicapping. But thoughts drowned in the pleasure rendered by her trained thumbs pressing at the small of my back.

"That's right," I gasped. "I've spent hours on a race and not cracked it. A player has to know when a race is unplayable and pass."

"Do you like betting on fillies or colts?"

There it was again. Only players know horse terms for girl and guy horses.

"Colts and geldings. Like the male of any species, they're easier to comprehend and have less complex motives." Her elbow came rattling up to the left side of my spine and I felt as if I was about to split open.

"Sprints or routes?"

It was certain she knew the game. Who cared. Her thumbs made mincemeat of the tight flesh to either side of my backbone.

"All depends on the track, the way the track is playing, inside or outside bias, composition, moisture content, race profile... and my mood."

"How about speed?"

"A key angle. But of course, you know that."

She dug her thumbs into my neck. My scream was involuntary. Her face was close to mine. I smelled apples and wine.

"I like you, do you know that, horseplayer?" she whispered, lips touching my ear. Goosebumps zinged from the base of my neck down my arms.

"I like you too," I said.

"That's good. Now roll over."

I did so with difficulty. My back felt like Riverdance had just been performed on it. On Matinee Day. She pumped a plunger on a bottle of baby oil, rubbed the grease into her hands, and straddled me at the ankles.

"How about layoffs?" she asked, running each hand up and

down my leg, just missing my genitals with her thumbs.

"An important part of the game, misunderstood by most, ignored by many. Layoffs tell the secret story of the horse." I was panting like I had just done a dozen windsprints.

"And the trainer?"

"Know the trainer, know the horse."

"Do you like when I do this?" She reduced the pressure and ran her long nails lightly up and down my legs.

"Oh yeah," I moaned.

"Size of the field. Does that matter?"

"Big fields confuse most players. They see lots of horses and figure lots of contenders. They lose the will to handicap the race. The truth is that in any race there are rarely more than three or four contenders. Of course, the bigger the field the more you need racing luck. That's why clearing speed is a plus in a big field."

"And horses jumping up in class?" She gently played with the pubic hairs on either side of my nutsack.

"A top angle," I gasped. "One of the best bets in the world and one you can make a living from. Wait for a jumpup with backclass who you suspect is returning to form and bet out."

"And how about this."

She moved up my legs and cupped my testicles in one hand and grabbed my penis with the other. She kissed my legs and I was rock hard and pulsing with blood glee and she gently put me inside her…

…and yet all I could see, with my eyes tightly closed, going around and around in my head, were horses.

Horses. Going round and around.

CHAPTER THIRTY - SEVEN

I thought it was morning although I wasn't sure. I thought about my evening with Ricki. Remorse and concern filled me. Now I was having unprotected sex with prostitutes. And how did she know so much about horse racing?

I stopped into the motel office to see if Mitra wanted to run a game of gin. A thin, Indian man with the name "Sahdi Singh" on a tag pinned to his shirt stood behind the desk.

"Where's Mitra?" I asked.

"Mitra is at the doctor, sir. May I be of help?"

"Is she alright?"

"Who is asking, sir?"

"My name is Sid. In room sixteen. Mitra and I are, ah, friends."

"Ah, Mr. Sidney, I have heard her speak of you. You are the Master of Gin."

"Hardly."

"I am her husband. She is in the hospital for tests. Apparently she ate something that disagreed with her."

"Not a pepperoni stick." He looked confused.

"It's a thin piece of spicy meat," I said.

"I doubt it sir. Mitra eats only the vegetables."

I breathed a sigh of relief and backed out of the office. The

Neon took me to a restaurant on Sunset Boulevard called The Griddle. I had read a review of the place. The pancakes were supposed to be the best in town.

They were huge. Even I had trouble finishing. With coffee the bill was over ten bucks. Too much for even big pancakes. Not too much to put on a 10-1 shot, though.

I drove around aimlessly, conscious of time bringing me closer to first post. The accepting, omnipotent racetrack. What was it about the track that kept me going in circles?

Circles. Like the horses in my head. My session with Ricki had triggered a non-stop horserace in my mind. I was rooting for one of the nags to win. Not sure which one. Every race was too close to call. The need to win was profound.

I found myself at a hardware store in West Hollywood with the narrowest aisles ever. I bought a shovel, rake, and trowel.

"Do you like gardening?" the cashier asked.

"Not really. Why do you ask?"

She shrugged and took my cash.

I drove to the track and parked the Neon in the furthest portion of the lot near the stable gate. I turned on a classical music station, put the seat back, listened, and dozed until it got dark. When it was pitch black I lifted the tools out of the trunk and casually made my way to a fence which separated the parking lot from the racetrack. About four hundred yards up on the right sat the huge, silent grandstand. I threw the tools over the fence. They landed with a thud on a dirt path which led from the stables to the paddock. I clambered over the fence with adrenaline fueled ease, ripping my pants in a couple of places. Once inside, I hid in bushes listening to insects converse and waited for my heart to stop pounding. It took a while.

I crawled on my hands and knees down a small dirt decline to the asphalt apron of the track. Cradling the tools to my chest I crouched and ran to a wooden fence that abutted the track. I slithered underneath. I was at the far turn, the part of the racetrack horses swung around as they entered the home stretch.

I stood in the middle of the track. The artificial surface was soft. I practically bounced over it, sinking slightly into the polymer fragments. I tapped the shovel on the track, feeling for a hollow spot.

I knew this was something many agencies had no doubt done but it didn't matter. I moved backwards around the turn, tapping as I went, to the quarter pole, the point at which there was a quarter mile to the finish. As I worked my way to the six furlong marker I heard a car screech to a halt. I ran across the track and threw myself into a narrow aluminum drainage ditch between the artificial surface and the turf course.

I peered up and saw a yellow security van stopped outside the fence, about eighty feet away at the crest of a small hill. A light played through the fence, a sharp, powerful beam, like a police spotlight. It meandered across the surface of the track and wended its way towards me.

I burrowed my head into the moldy spine of the drainage tube. I sensed the light playing on my jacket. My muscles begged for release. I remained frozen, listening to an inner scream.

A car engine finally roared to life. I heard the vehicle pull away. I looked up. I was alone. Holding a shovel. An implement with which I might well be digging my own grave.

CHAPTER THIRTY - EIGHT

I guess I must have fallen asleep. When I woke up the sky was ablaze with early morning pink. I was looking up at the underside of what looked to be a large bush. As I did not recall having a plant in my room at The Surf, I was momentarily disoriented. Then the bush began talking.

"Sid, even for you, this is strange behavior," the bush said.

I wondered if I should respond. Why not, I talk to my imaginary brother.

"What's strange?" I asked.

"Breaking into the track with a bunch of gardening tools. Doing a little midnight landscaping?"

The voice was sonorous and deep. Like the Moses bush. It had a familiar ring.

"Not a great idea," I said. "Not sure what I was thinking."

"It's time for you to get serious," said the bush. "Do what you were born to do."

"Which is?"

I watched the bush for a response. It was a big bush, almost like a tiny tree. Maybe it was a tiny tree. Little funnels of yellow flowers adorned the spindly branches. Minty colored leaves rustled in the morning wind. Perhaps the bush was clearing its throat. I was about to repeat myself when a figure in a cowboy hat stepped out from behind it.

"Lemmons. How did you know I was here?"

"A friend of mine in security saw you hiding in a drainage ditch last night. You're lucky he called me and not the Inglewood PD. They like to use their tasers, I'm told."

"I thought I got away with it."

"Got away?" asked Lemmons. "Everybody from the track publicity office to the LA Times to the LAPD knows John's older brother Sidney is out here checking things out. Since you spend most of your time at the motel playing gin it hasn't been an issue. Digging a hole in the racetrack has people viewing you in a new light."

"Which is?"

"That you're a major league wack job."

I sat up and stretched. Every bone in my body hurt.

"Morning workouts over?" I asked

"For almost an hour." He nodded at three huge tractors pulling harrows that traveled in a counter clockwise direction around the track. "They're grooming the surface for the afternoon's races."

"You have anything going?"

"Princess Bride in the 7th."

I tensed.

"Just kidding," Lemmons said. "You should see your face. Like you seen a ghost. You hungry?"

"Starving."

"Good. Let's get some hot links and eggs over in the pantry. Have another chat about horserace handicapping."

"I don't think so," I said.

"Why not?"

"It's too much for me. Handicapping is a tough game when one's head is screwed on straight. The way mine is? Forget it."

"I'm a patient man," said Lemmons. "Have to be. When you're training horses, especially bad ones, no matter how you try to get them to the races, God has other plans. A shin splint, pulled muscle, thrown shoe, a touch of colic. You never know. Humans have a bit more say in the matter. Free will and all."

I slowly got to my feet. I was standing in the infield of

Hollywood Park having a conversation with a horse trainer. A couple of curious flamingos with nothing better to do regarded us from a small lake.

"See you later, Bob." I turned and walked away.

"Sid," Lemmons called. "You gonna take your gardening tools?"

CHAPTER THIRTY - NINE

It was as easy as a tiny idea. Which I had while driving up La Brea after my night in the Hollywood Park infield and my meeting with Lemmons. It was to play a couple of games of pool at a local watering hole I had observed on a street named Holloway. An inviting little joint by the name of Barney's Beanery.

I hung a left on Stockard and drove west to La Cienega, then north, past fast foot joints, upscale restaurants, middle-eastern rug stores, trendy clubs, and on to Holloway, where I made a right. There was a parking spot in front of Barney's.

I walked up to the bartender to get change for the pool table. She was a pretty young woman with a large stone dangling from a silver chain in the middle of her belly button, which was exposed, as was most of her mid section, by a halter top made for a five year old. I got my quarters and looked around the place. "Satisfaction" by the Stones was blaring away on a passable sound system. I walked over to the furthest pool table, popped in eight quarters, and started smacking the balls around. I longed to play somebody, feel the joy of competition. I imagined the beautiful bartender asking me for a game. Maybe that wasn't it. Maybe it wasn't about pool. Maybe I was here for one reason.

Maybe I had a thirst.

A powerful thirst that needed quenching. Nothing to do with

desire or need. It was beyond that. Something so primordial as to be inexpressible. It bubbled within me like a lifeless pool, without form, that needed filling. An amalgam of dark voices so interwoven that it became the fabric, the template, of all I might be.

I needed a drink, was all.

I approached the bar. Barney's smelled like beer. Beer from eight thousand spilled pitchers permeated every inch of the place. This joint was the temple of broken dreams. As I neared the bar it was the moment of truth. I glanced at the door. The light beckoned. I kept on to the bar. I yearned to run. Into my Neon. And go where?

Back to my seedy motel room and watch HBO until my money ran out? Meditate on the nothingness my life had become? To New York and to my dead end life? Writing bullshit scripts? To the track to handicap horses?

I heard the self pity in the appraisal and knew it impelled me to the booze but I could do nothing about it.

"What do you have on tap," I asked the beautiful bartender. It would please her if I drank. It is what people do in places like this. She would appreciate it if I hunkered down with an ice cold pitcher at 9:30 in the morning. I would drink like a man and act like a man and be a man.

"Oh, about fifty different brews, ice cold from the tap."

A pearl glistened from the middle of her little pink tongue.

"What would you recommend?" I asked.

"You look like a Budwesier man."

Sure, I thought. A little souse. A ne'er do well. A little slouch of a daddy who never was.

"That's fine," I said. "A pitcher of Bud. Large." She drew it, handed it to me along with a frosted glass. I gave her a ten, told her to keep the change. She thanked me profusely. I resisted the urge to run into the bathroom to count my money. It wouldn't be enough, that's for sure.

I brought the pitcher and glass over to a table in the corner. I stared at the pitcher. The little bubbles seemed driven upwards by a pump from the bottom of the pitcher. I smelled damp relief in the amber liquid.

116

CHAPTER FORTY

There was no rumination before the first sip. Not like years before. Back then, as I sat in my taxi with a bottle of Labatt's in my hand, I asked God's will be done. Then I could not lift the bottle to my mouth. The hand of God was heavy on my arm. God was with me. Not at Barney's. Maybe there was no God in Los Angeles.

After my first sip of booze in over four years there was no bolt of lightning. I glanced around Barney's. Nobody seemed to notice this pivotal moment in humanity. After the first glass the world took on a rosy glow. There was hope. I was the master of my ship, Captain of my destiny.

After the second pitcher the Captain lost control of the vessel. I vaguely remembered heaving my pool cue against the wall after losing a $5 game of Eight-Ball to a construction worker and then asking the cute bartender if she was attracted to me. Shortly thereafter I was escorted out of Barney's by a portly grey-haired manager with a vice-grip on my right ear.

The clock on the dash of the Neon said 1:10. I had been in Barney's less than two hours. I felt like going to the track but my stake was too low. Resentment coursed within me. I was in a bad place with no exit. The rosy hope of the first glass of Bud was a distant memory.

I drove around LA, cutting people off. I was a fiend on

wheels. Someone was tailing me? I jammed on my brakes. Failed to signal? I tailgated them, horn blaring. I was my own Middle East, spreading tension and discord wherever I went. After I tailgated a Lexus SUV for a couple of blocks, I pulled alongside at a red light just outside the Beverly Center.

"Fuck you," I yelled into the Lexus. I was dimly aware the driver was a chiseled young dude with a tattoo of an eagle on a bulging bicep. "And suck my dick," I added, reaching toward the glove compartment.

He just stared at me.

"I'll fuck you up," I screamed.

I opened the glove compartment. Inside was a Neon car manual and a box of Tic Tacs. I grabbed the box of Tic Tacs and thrust it into my belt as if it was a gun. As I did, the Lexus-dude got out, walked slowly to his trunk, removed a tire iron, and strolled up to the back window on my side.

"Hey, wait a minute!" I yelled. It was too late. The crowbar smashed into the plate-glass. Without waiting for another swing from this hormone riddled animal, I jerked the Neon to the right, barely missing a Latino nanny guiding a Caucasian baby in a stroller. I accelerated south to the light at 3rd and La Cienega, looped around a line of cars, zoomed west on third and, without stopping, sailed through the light on San Vicente, heading north. I furtively glanced in my rear view but my attacker was nowhere to be found. Glass was all over the place. A pen-sized shard of glass was lodged in my left forearm and blood streamed from a deep gash. At Beverly I made a u-turn and headed south to The Surf.

I parked and marched into the lobby to find Mitra and her husband seated side by side. He was feeding her a green substance from a small Tupperware container. She appeared to have lost a couple of pounds, making her nose appear larger, if that was possible.

"Mr. Sid, it is good to see you," she said brightly. She took a better look. "Uh-oh, you seem to be under the influence."

"Fuck me and fuck you," I said. "I need my money. What is it, five hundred dollars?"

"Five hundred and twenty-one," she said. "Why don't you

lie down and we will talk afterwards."

"Don't fuck with me," I screamed. She wasn't a two hundred pound maniac with a tire iron. "I'm the King of Los Angeles. Do not FUCK with me!"

Mitra remained serene. Perhaps there was even a small smile playing around her mouth. I felt a need to smash her Indian face in. I glanced at her husband. He was glaring at me. The force of his hated knocked me back a couple of steps.

"I'm sorry," I stuttered. I backed out of the lobby and stumbled to my room. I threw myself on my bed and passed out.

CHAPTER FORTY - ONE

I awoke to a spinning room. Perhaps the earth had accelerated its rate of revolution while I was sleeping off my first drunk in over two years.

Vague recollections swam into my consciousness. Being thrown out of Barney's. Wild driving. The tire iron maniac. Insulting Mitra. Beautiful Mitra, my soul-Indian love teacher, Goddess of Yoo Hoo and divine mediation. I saw myself at Hollywood Park, yelling, screaming. What a hellacious piece of shit I was. Alone in a motel in LA. Further away from finding my brother than ever.

It dawned on me that I had to find myself in order to find my brother. This revelation was followed by a nausea so profound that it felt as if my spleen was swimming north through my gullet and into my mouth. I almost made it to the porcelain altar when waves of barely digested Budweiser, the King of Barf, came pouring out my mouth and onto the bathroom floor.

After the first salvo, I knelt clinging to the toilet, feeling relief until the next burst. I seemed to have more liquid within me than Lake Erie. I spent an infinity expelling the poison of a serious binge. When there was no more bile to spew I crawled back to the bed. I managed to clamber up onto the defiled bedspread, knowing the end was imminent.

It may have been a Godsend. It may have been the end of

passivity. It may have been the end of a man longing for things he wants but does nothing to get. It may have been the end of reason, reason calculated to keep a human comfortable for as long as possible on this earth, caring not for the accomplishments that occur not at all and are regretted in the rabid moments before death. It may have been the end of shallow intimations of love expected but not rendered, of demons who cared not who they hurt or whose lives they tore asunder.

It may have been the end of me. With that oddly reassuring thought I fell into a deep sleep.

CHAPTER FORTY - TWO

When I awoke Mitra was by the side of the bed.

"How are you doing?" she asked.

"Ugh."

"You were very sick," she said.

"How long?"

"Three days."

"Three days?"

"Oh yes. You returned from The Barney's with a full head of steam. Since then you have gone to the track and always with a head of beer. There was no stopping you."

"Three days," I said. I raised my anvil of a head and glanced around the room. The floor was carpeted with losing race track tickets and empty cans of Budweiser. I groaned inwardly as the nimble fingers of nascent nausea massaged my esophagus.

"Are you going to heave ho?" asked Mitra.

"I don't think so. I've got to do something, Mitra. In my whole life I've never taken a chance. I'm not talking about betting $400 on a 20-1 shot."

"But that is over $8,000, a handsome fee even in these United States."

It struck me odd that she did the calculation so quickly. But so many things had been weird on this trip.

"I've got to figure out where to start," I said.

"I know where," said Mitra. "You must start at the conclusion. You must see the end clearly with your own bloodshot eyes. Willing to make the choice while knowing your fate."

"What are you talking about?" I said. "Look, I'm sorry for the things I said the other night."

"That bothers me not, Mr. Sid. We are friends, older friends than even our brief time together on this mortal plane. However, you might want to give my husband a box of candies. He is protective and a tad upset. He enjoys the See's. The vanilla lollipops. You will find the factory store straight down La Cienega."

"I can barely afford it," I said. "I didn't have much money before the spree."

"You have $3 left. Mostly quarters. A chip and a chair. That is all you need. Do you not watch the poker on TV? Exhilarating!"

"What am I going to do with $3?" I was feeling dry. A little thirsty. "Is there a can of beer lying around?"

"All empty, thanks Dharma," she said. "You must do nothing for several days but drink broth and consider your new path. It is time for you to live your true purpose."

"My what?"

She extended a three by five card to me. I took it. On it was written:

> Charles Lackey
> 40 Trellis Lane
> Victorville, CA

The name was vaguely familiar but I couldn't place it.

"After you dry out you will go in your rental car to see Mr. Charles Lackey. On that journey the end of your days will be revealed and thus your beginning as well."

"Whatever you say, Mitra."

She pulled a deck of cards out of one sweatshirt pocket and a fistful of bills from the other.

"Here is the $521 I owe you," she said. "That is yours. You beat me fair and square. But now I have you in the weakened state."

"My sweet Indian rose," I said, taking the money. "If I was brain dead and attached to tubes I'd still whip you."

"We shall see, Mr. Sid. Let us cut for deal."

CHAPTER FORTY - THREE

I spent the next three days in The Surf sleeping, playing cards with Mitra and drinking a savory, rose-tasting broth she provided. I wasn't very hungry. Maybe I had a fever for I had odd dreams. In them was a deity on a throne. I felt nurtured and loved. Beneath this God's feet, running about, were my mother and father, faces attached to rodent bodies.

I managed to beat Mitra for another $120. She wanted to pay but I declined. I felt it was bad form to collect a bet from someone who has saved your life.

One morning I left the room for the first time in almost a week. Mitra and I walked arm and arm down La Cienega, east on Packard and continued for about half an hour. Sunlight streamed through the reedy autumn air, splashing onto the cracked pavement and spreading pools of damp light at our feet. When we returned to The Surf I was tired. The craving for booze was gone. I noticed the window in the Neon was repaired.

Later that night, I took a drive to the See's store on La Cienega and picked up a fistful of vanilla lollipops. I drove back, made sure the lobby was empty and left them behind the desk. I couldn't think of anything to put on a note so I didn't.

Early the next morning I dressed and put the 3x5 card in my shirt pocket. Mitra had done my laundry. I drove south on La

Cienega to an Exxon station, filled, and plotted my journey to Victorville using a Thomas Guide from a rack. I bought a couple of bananas for breakfast, my first solid food in three days.

I picked up the 10 East and within minutes was streaking past the puny LA downtown skyline. Few cars were heading in my direction. West was another matter. Extending as far as the eye could see was a long line of fuming cars and trucks. Faces of disconsolate drivers were like prisoners in jail cells.

I took the freeway to the 15 North. Signs pointed to Barstow and Las Vegas. The words Las Vegas produced a tingle in my groin. Once on the 15 Freeway I headed north through cow country and small pockets of newly built condos. They seemed to be uninhabited. As I continued north these clusters of buildings thinned out until it was mostly desert. Parched land extended to distant mountains, broken only by an occasional cactus or scrub bush. The Thomas guide told me to exit at D Street in Victorville. I finally got there and made a left.

There was little along D Street except an occasional tire repair store, strawberry stand or home-style restaurant. According to the map, Trellis Lane was about five miles east of the freeway. I passed a couple of unmarked dirt roads. Maybe one of them was Trellis. Who could say? This was desolate territory. Mangy dogs ran in packs behind deserted buildings. For sale signs hung on clapboard houses set back from D Street. Huge billboards announced Indian Casinos or Comfort Inns. A large, modern building, the Purple Rooster Gentlemen's Club, appeared like a neon- festooned mirage. About forty cars were parked in a huge asphalt u-shaped lot.

I almost missed Trellis Lane. A small sign dangled from a small pole just beyond the Purple Rooster. I veered left and took the turn.

Trellis Lane was unpaved, about ten feet wide and abutted by a deep, dry gully on either side. An occasional horse or cow nibbled at saw grass. Crows swooped overhead, lazily checking out the daily specials.

Just when I thought I was lost, Trellis Lane opened into a trailer park. A sign said IMMILMAN'S – REPORT TO OFFICE. A

126

slight downgrade led to a large dirt parking lot, behind which were trailers set apart at fifty foot intervals. Some had satellite dishes hanging from roofs or windows. Clothes hung on ropes between the trailers. The only sign of life was a small child throwing a Frisbee aimlessly against the side of a trailer. He looked up at me. I waved. He looked away and continued his game.

The trailers were marked sequentially. I decided not to check in at the office. Trellis Lane widened slightly. The further I went the more the land behind the trailer park was desert. I followed the road as mailbox numbers ascended until, at a fork, I noticed an arrow pointing to spaces, 32-40.

The trailers got larger, more ornate. This was the Boardwalk and Park Place of Immilman's. Number 40 was set off under a large stand of fir and eucalyptus. The trailer was a modern and looked like a huge aluminum cigar tube. Lawn chairs, a chaise lounge, and a Weber Barbeque were outside. I parked, got out and stretched. The mailbox said LACKEY.

I looked around. The kid with the Frisbee was about fifty yards away. I smiled. The kid spit into the dust and moved out of sight behind a trailer.

I moved toward space number 40. Mitra had sent me here.
Mitra.
If not for her, I would be long gone.

CHAPTER FORTY - FOUR

I knocked on the door for a while. No response. I sat on the chaise lounge looking south at trailers sprouting out of the earth like mushrooms. Frisbee kid hadn't made a return appearance. I wondered how long I was supposed to sit here. The sun filtered through the eucalyptus, warm against my face.

I must have fallen asleep for I awakened to the gravelly sound of a man's voice.

"Who the hell are you?"

I opened my eyes. An old man stood over me. His few wisps of grey hair waved lazily in the breeze. A bloated face featured several days worth of gray stubble. He was dressed like a refugee from a Catskills Hotel: faded yellow Polo shirt, madras walking shorts, black knee high socks, and white Bally loafers. A good-sized paunch pushed the Polo shirt inches from my face. A pastiness about him made me think of pizza dough.

"Mitra sent me."

"Who?"

"Mitra. From the Surf Motel."

"The Surf Motel. Is it in Miami?"

"No. On La Cienega in LA."

"I haven't been in LA in years."

I got to my feet. "You are Mr. Charles Lackey?"

He nodded. He was about five-eight with decent posture. A hint of former gentility in his mien. He regarded me through clear eyes.

"I'm not the Charles Lackey you want to know."

"Well then, I'll be on my way."

"Good idea," he said. He turned and shuffled wearily toward the trailer. Slipped the key into the lock. *Click.* A recollection popped into my consciousness.

"Excuse me, Mr. Lackey. Are you the guy who won the World Series of Handicapping two years in a row, in 2002 and 2003?" He turned, faced me.

"How would you know about that?"

"I played those contests," I said. "Came in twenty-seventh in 2003. Thought I recognized you."

"Yeah, I'm that Charles Lackey," he said. "You're a fellow player, are you?"

"Oh no, Mr. Lackey. I'm nobody. You're a player. "

This was true. The odds were astronomical against winning the World Series once. Two years in a row was like hitting the Lottery back to back.

"That's kind of you," he said, "although it wasn't that difficult."

"I played in 2004," I said. "You didn't play that year."

"No," he said. "2003 was my last hurrah." Something told me not to press him.

"A horseplayer," he said with a smile. "I haven't talked handicapping for a long time."

"Neither have I," I said.

"Why not?"

"Kind of gave up the game."

"Let your passion get the best of you," he said.

"I'm not sure what happened."

"You're looking defeated, son."

"What makes you say that?"

"It's coming through your pores. The sweat of a million losses, real or imagined. You've been short-circuited, my young friend."

"You just met me."

"You think I'd say two words to you if I just met you? I know you like I know myself."

I wanted to argue but I was too tired.

"What do you want to do?" he asked.

"What do you mean?"

"Do you want to play the horses?"

I looked at the ground. Squibs of leaves were carted about by tiny red ants. It didn't seem possible the ants could hold such a burden.

"You don't have any idea what it takes, do you, son."

"I guess not."

"That's honest. How about some macaroni and cheese. Come on in and we'll find out what's what and what's not."

CHAPTER FORTY - FIVE

I couldn't remember the last time I was inside a trailer. To my right was a small kitchen featuring a refrigerator and microwave oven. A threadbare green cloth couch was in front of me. Behind it was a small window partially covered with a white curtain. To my left and occupying most of the trailer was a desk on which sat a laptop. Facing the desk on the wall were five medium-sized plasma TV sets. Beyond that strings of bamboo partitioned the main body of the trailer from what I assumed were Lackey's sleeping quarters and bathroom.

"I've been here about five years," Lackey said. "Hope you don't mind if I don't dress for lunch, ha ha."

He moved into the kitchen. Out of the corner of my eye I saw the TV screens flicker to life. As the pictures swam into focus I saw each featured a different racetrack. It was like being in a Vegas sports book. Outside the little window the sun was burning bright in a blue sky. The microwave went on with a pop. I saw a plastic dish spinning lazily inside.

"It's about 10:30 so we'll be getting Aqueduct, Hawthorne, Churchill, Laurel and Calder. Later we'll pick up the western tracks. I don't bet much these days. You want something to drink?"

I realized he had never asked my name.

"Water's fine."

"I'm going to have me a beer," he said. "I love beer. I know I shouldn't be drinking but I'm too old to care. What do you care about?"

"I don't know."

"Jesus, you're too young not to know what you care about. Later on it sort of happens."

I went over and sat on the couch. Glanced at the TV sets. There was something calming about the place.

"The key is permission," Lackey said. "Conflict will fuck you up. It's okay if you're a tortured artist. That's what artistic creativity demands. There's no room for internal conflict in sports or war. If you're a horseplayer or soldier you're either one hundred percent present or you're dead or broke. I'm not sure which is worse."

Lackey brought me a steaming bowl of macaroni and cheese. It smelled great. For the first time in what seemed weeks I was really hungry. I looked down at Lackey's toenails and was shocked to see they were manicured and coated with a shiny, clear polish.

"One of my few affectations," he grinned sheepishly. "Eat up, son. You're going to need your strength."

CHAPTER FORTY - SIX

The macaroni and cheese was delicious. Lackey had a coffee maker that operated when a little canister was placed in a holder and punched open. It was strong and good. We sat on the couch and I told him my story. He wanted to hear all the details of my handicapping career.

As I talked, Lackey slumped lower on the couch. I figured he was bored, except every time I tried to speed up he would motion for me to slow down. When his eyes began closing and I was convinced he was asleep he would ask a question and I knew he was listening.

When I was finished I looked at my watch. I couldn't believe I'd been yammering for the better part of two hours. I waited for some reaction. Lackey's eyelids were at half-mast. He was breathing heavily. Then he started wheezing. He grabbed his chest, lurched to his feet and staggered through the bamboo curtains. When he came back he was pale but steady.

"I usually feel it coming on," he said. "Sorry you had to see it. I'm going to rest for a while. The couch pulls out to a comfortable bed. The sheets are fresh and there's a quilt in the cabinet over the microwave. I'll be up in time for dinner. I know you're wondering what the hell is going on. Considering the last few months I'd have thought you might have stopped asking that question. I'll tell you anyway. For the first time in your life every action will matter. You think you've told me about yourself? You haven't. What a person remembers is irrelevant. It's about intention in the moment. You don't have to respond. I know you don't understand. You can leave at any time. But you won't. I'll see you later."

He shuffled off to the bedroom. I sat on the couch for a while. A powerful fatigue rendered me senseless. Out of the corner of my eye the races were playing on five screens. Somewhere a horseplayer was getting rich, many more were broken, and all by the same dream. I laid down on the couch, tucked a cushion under my head, and fell asleep.

CHAPTER FORTY - SEVEN

When I opened my eyes it was dark. Lackey was at the desk staring at one of the screens. He was dressed in a white dress shirt, black pants and loafers.

"You hungry?" he asked.

"Yeah." I was famished.

Lackey drove an old Toyota Corolla. We took the 15 freeway north a couple of exits and wound up at a place called Sylvia's. It was a small, comfortable joint, maybe fifteen round tables with checked linen covers. The air was rich with the smell of grilled meats. Most of the tables were occupied by families. A pretty hostess came over.

"Mr. L, good to see you," she gushed.

"Same here, sweetheart. Leslie, this is my prodigy, Sid Rubin. Sid, this is Leslie, daughter of Sylvia. There really was a Sylvia before she retired with her millions to Boynton Beach in Florida."

Leslie extended a hand. When I took it and looked into her crystal blue eyes I realized I hadn't held a woman's hand in a friendly way for a long time. She led us to a table in the corner and left.

We examined the menus. When the waitress arrived Lackey said, "We'll have the king filets, rare, mashed potatoes, gravy, sautéed mushrooms, creamed spinach and maybe a couple of shrimp cocktails to start off. Beer for me and a can of Coke for the boy genius."

When she left Lackey said, "Hope you don't mind me ordering. I like going out to dinner. It reminds me of being human." He opened his napkin and placed it in his lap.

"Most horseplayers inhabit a world of illusion," he continued. "The average player experiences incessant pain and loss and keeps playing. Some people say it is obsessive behavior but I don't think so. Those who are obsessed are tormented by the experience. Horseplayers are nurtured by it. It's a world of hope until the money runs out."

"You were successful," I said. "You won the World Series two years in a row."

"I also won ten out of eleven smaller tournaments in between. Most people forget about that. "

"You must have lost that one because of bad racing luck. Anything can happen in a race."

"That's not true," said Lackey. "When one is handicapping on the highest level one is not predicting the future, one is creating it. Let me repeat: when one is handicapping at the highest level one is not predicting the future, one is creating it. The way you handicap the race is the only way it can come out. "

"What about luck?"

"You only need, want, or expect luck if you're fearful. In the absence of fear lies the possibility of creation."

Our waitress appeared with two huge shrimp cocktails and a couple of bottles of beer and a can of Coke.

"Let's eat," said Lackey.

CHAPTER FORTY - EIGHT

For the first few weeks Lackey had me staring at the TV screens with the sound off. He would disappear for hours at a time. He said he liked walking in the desert. One morning while he was getting dressed I saw a white bag attached to his side. He told me it was a colostomy bag. Some years earlier after a bout with colon cancer much of his large intestine was removed. Between that and his wheezing I figured he had to be in some discomfort, though I never heard him complain.

There was something dreamlike about watching the races without sound and without racing data. At first I would fall asleep as if I was reading poetry that although beautiful was stultifying. Lackey told me this boredom was the vestige of the compulsive gambler in me dying. As the days went by and my eyes flicked from screen to screen I became immersed in the races. For the first time in my horse-playing life I wasn't trying to beat the races. It was amazing what happened when money was taken out of the equation. Speaking of which, Lackey never let me pay for a thing. He would make us sandwiches or pasta for lunch. For dinner we would go to Sylvia's or a local burger or pizza joint. Wherever we went Lackey slurped up his brew. I had no desire to drink.

I was virtually absent of desire. I had the urge to masturbate from time to time just to see if my "member of royalty" still worked but refrained. A part of me felt like a boxer in training. I wasn't sure what I was preparing for but it felt important.

CHAPTER FORTY - NINE

I seemed to have no recollection of past or anticipation or future. All was the moment and the races.

The raw power of the animals was mesmerizing, muscle laden torsos supported by spindly legs, going as fast and as long as they could. The horse with the fastest time would win. The world was spinning. Breath went in and out. Seasons changed, men and women fell in love, babies were born and old folks died and the cycle went on and on and where was the plan in it, the resolution of chance. I brought this up to Lackey over sausage pizza at his favorite Italian joint, Leo's, just outside of Victorville.

"I guess you're not learning much," said Lackey his mouth crammed with pizza. With his assortment of physical ailments Lackey seemed determined to go down eating.

"I was hoping by now you'd be doing a little less thinking," he continued. "Can't you see thinking's what's screwed you up so far?"

"I guess," I said.

"At some point you have to let go of the need to know. Horserace handicapping has knowledge at its root. But the key to success in this game is recognition borne of focus and intuition that transcends knowledge. Thinking interferes with that."

"Most people can't handicap," I said.

"And yet there are idiots who get lucky and connect with cap horse after cap horse. How do you think I lost that one tournament? They are in the minority, thank god. The vast majority of tournament horseplayers are doomed to mediocrity because of their extensive study of handicapping. They will arrive on their deathbeds confused, convinced as they were for years that the illusive prize was within their grasp. They had no idea they were doomed by the prison of computer programs, Beyer numbers, Ragozin sheets, Thorograph analysis and anything else that tried to quantify the unquantifiable. Pass the hot peppers."

I handed him the pepper bottle and watched in horror as he unscrewed the cap and sprinkled the deadly stuff across a slice of pizza.

"I know you have the knowledge, otherwise we wouldn't be having this conversation. I know you're a great handicapper, have all the skill it takes. We just have to get you to stop thinking and then, by god, you just might have a chance to forget who you are and make your mark on this godforsaken world."

I watched him eat, trying not to think.

"Jeez," he gasped, "I gotta buy some Tums on the way home."

CHAPTER FIFTY

The next morning Lackey wasn't at his usual place at the desk. When I got out of the bathroom he still wasn't around. I figured he was sleeping off the pizza. When I finished a bowl of Special K with whole milk and bananas and there was still no sight of him I peeked inside his bedroom. The bed was made and the room was empty.

I sat on the couch waiting. After a while I went over and turned on the TVs. A storm had swept up the coast and the tracks were wet, races were off the turf, and there were lots of scratches.

Almost on an inspiration I went and whipped open the trailer door expecting to see Lackey spying on me. There was nothing but the barbeque and chaise lounges. A brisk wind blew a Snicker's bar wrapper against the side of the trailer. The smell of frying bacon wafted in the air. It was cool and it was the whisper of winter. When I got cold I went back inside.

For lack of anything better to do I watched the races. I don't belong here, I thought. This wacky has-been has me watching horse races without sound. The guy doesn't even bet anymore. He's been reduced to living in a trailer, shitting into a bag and wheezing. I wondered how Debra was doing. And Tony, my AA sponsor. I needed somebody to talk to.

The urge to get off that chair was profound. They were leading the horses to the gate for the first race at Calder. There were only six of them, non-winners of three races running for a tag of $6,250. The favorite was 3-5. I wondered what he looked like in The Racing Form. The bell rang and they were off. The favorite was between horses early and involved in a testing speed duel. The jockey was looking from side to side. They were squeezing him coming to the turn. The other three horses were getting closer, moving as a team toward the embattled leaders. All the horses had chances. Approaching the eighth pole the favorite began to fade. A 22-1 shot surged up on the outside to win by a nose. God, that was a $46 dollar horse, or in contest parlance a "Cap" horse, a horse with the highest allowable payoff.

I was thinking about money. About what might have been. About the payoff that had nothing to do with the process. I turned my attention to the Aqueduct screen. The track was a sea of slop. A gray sky hung over the Queens skyline. A jet flew low, aiming for a runway at JFK. A seagull hopped three times and skittered into the infield lake. The horses for the first race were coming onto the track. The track. Where they would run and manifest what they were at that exact moment in time and the truth that no loneliness could touch.

CHAPTER FIFTY - ONE

Lackey was gone the next day, too. I made myself a cup of coffee and some instant oatmeal. It was too early for the East Coast races. I borrowed one of Lackey's warm coats and a set of keys and went outside. I walked toward the end of the trailer park. I didn't see a soul. About fifty yards beyond the last trailer the silent desert opened up. The packed dirt was peppered with scrub grass, ragged bushes, and weeds as far as the eye could see. I walked straight into it. It was a lot of prehistoric nothing except for flies that buzzed me. After a half hour my head was as barren as the landscape. I could see why Lackey liked walking in it.

Lackey wasn't there when I got back. I hung up his coat and turned on the races. I didn't know what else to do. I thought of heading back to LA or New York or calling the police or the local hospital. I couldn't figure out why he hadn't told me he was leaving unless it was an emergency.

Then something occurred to me.

Maybe I wasn't supposed to figure anything out. This had nothing to do with Lackey. It had to do with me and horse race handicapping. Lackey's question flashed back at me, the question to which I had no answer a few days before:

What did I want to do?

I wanted to handicap horse races. I wanted to explore the

data, feel the information, have it become a living thing in my brain. I wanted to push through the loneliness, insecurity, immaturity and whatever else had set me up for years of booze and gambling riddled insanity. I wanted to appreciate the subtlety of a horse race, uncover the angles, interpret the data correctly and experience the dissolution of the desire to do well.

Lackey was a catalyst for the process. Whether he returned was unimportant. Perhaps my brother had to disappear so I might appear.

I watched the races all day without a thought of winning and losing. I didn't stop for lunch and I wasn't aware the races were over until the screens were running test signals. Somehow the hypnosis broke and I got up from the desk.

Lackey was sitting on the couch.

"Well done," he said. "It's time to move on."

CHAPTER FIFTY - TWO

We were finishing breakfast the next day when Lackey said, "Take a look around. This is what you'll end up with. A broken body and a life at the end of the world. If you're lucky you'll have an interest in handicapping. Everything else will have been burned away by the fire of your errant interest. Is this what you want?"

"Just because we're both handicappers doesn't mean I have to end up like you."

"No," said Lackey. "But you will. It has to do with what's inside here." Lackey tapped his forehead. "If you live inside your head long enough the heart shrivels. It keeps pumping but the brain recognizes it only as a physical entity. Your soul dies. You become a mutant. You have a chance to turn back before the wiring becomes permanent."

"I thought that's why you left me by myself. To see if the desire was there."

"You don't get it," said Lackey. "I don't do anything. Everything you do is an act of free will. Until you make horse race handicapping your path."

I wasn't sure what he was talking about.

"Do you know how I felt when I won the World Series for the first time?" Lackey asked. "Guys were coming up to me and pumping my hand. Some dude from ESPN had a microphone in my face. They handed me a check for $350,000. The place was going crazy. In photos I look like I just got out of bed. You know those moments when dreams are pounding away but the reality of the day intrudes? That's what it felt like. I was annoyed that people were wrenching me from a restful state into chaos. I tried to be humble and say the right things. In that moment of glory there wasn't one thing I wanted to do except review the day's races. To see what I missed. My former wife called. Supposedly to congratulate me. She and her new boyfriend were struggling. She ripped my heart out when she left. I sent her a hundred grand."

I stared at Lackey, searching for something to say.

"You don't know nothing about nothing," he said. "I hope you never do. Tomorrow we'll start looking at the Racing Form."

CHAPTER FIFTY - THREE

When I came out of the bathroom the next day Lackey was at the desk, a Racing Form in front of him. It was about a half hour before the first race at Laurel in Maryland. There was another Racing Form on the couch. I assumed it was for me. I got a cup of coffee, sat down and picked it up. I read a couple of articles and turned to the races from Hollywood. I tried to handicap a low level claiming event but got tired. My head nodded and the form slipped out of my fingers.

"That's what comes from trying," said Lackey.

"I wasn't trying," I said.

"I could feel it. I glanced over and your hands were gripping the paper like a bad driver a steering wheel. You were trying to figure out the winner without appreciation for the story."

"How is one supposed to handicap without trying?"

"You've got to have the innocence of a child, the energy of an adolescent, the knowledge of an adult and the intuition of an old man. Kids don't try to have fun. They just do. When they try, like in school, they get bored."

"How does one regain innocence?"

"By floating above the object of desire. By interacting with the Racing Form without expectation."

I stared blankly at Lackey.

He sighed. "God, you're a project. I'll say it again: this isn't about me. As long as it is you're doomed to be a failure and, worse, a big pain in my ass."

Lackey had me pull a chair over and watch him the rest of the day. He went race after race without moving a muscle, studying the form, glancing up at the TVs and back again.

"Patience is a key. Remember, you're not predicting the future, you're creating it. You're not God or whatever Universal Intelligence you believe is responsible for this earthly mayhem. You are patient, accruing energy, every once in a while generating truth."

"I haven't seen you make a bet," I said.

"I told you, I don't bet often. The process takes too much effort. In case you haven't noticed I need most of my energy to keep breathing. I'm sure I've overlooked opportunities I wouldn't have missed a few years ago. It's important not to become frustrated when you miss a bet. The rest of the handicappers in any tournament are threats only in the moment of your frustration. Otherwise they don't exist."

Suddenly Lackey's posture became rigid. His eyes flicked back and forth from the Aqueduct screen to the Racing Form.

"This is interesting," he said. "The nine horse is 14-1. You know that feeling, don't you, Sid, the energy that accompanies insight?"

He tapped away on the keyboard. "I'm too old for this," he said. "But I thought it was important you see that prediction has nothing to do with the act of creation."

CHAPTER FIFTY - FOUR

The horse won and paid $33. Lackey had bet $200 to win and $3,300 was deposited into his account. I watched his face during the running of the race. It was an impassive as if he was eating toast.

"I almost wish the horse lost," he said. When I asked what he meant he waved me off. The rest of the day Lackey lectured me on the general nature of horse race handicapping. I felt lucky to be listening to the best handicapper ever to open a Racing Form.

"I'm going to tell you things you already know," said Lackey. "However, you may feel as if you're hearing things for the first time. That's because words acquire meaning when emanating from a higher consciousness. I'm not talking about me." He grinned and pointed upward.

"A good bet can come from any race at any track. This is a hard thing to deal with when one is in a contest and you have as many as eight racetracks to handicap. How can you handicap seventy races and process the information properly? The computer boys who quantify information might have an edge. What they gain in numbers management they lose in intuitive gold. A lot depends on your night-before handicapping. You must ascertain whether every race has a false favorite the night before. You must do this without handicapper selections. You must use only the information in the Racing Form. Follow?"

"Of course."

"Night before handicapping is not easy when you are in a contest. You will be exhausted after a day of competition. That is if you're playing well. If you're not bone-tired after a contest day you should take that extra energy and get on a plane and go home. Oh yeah, did I mention eating? You never eat on the day of a contest."

"No food?" I asked.

"Very little," said Lackey. "An occasional hard candy to keep the glucose level up. That's it. The greatest sight in the world is watching fat contest handicappers belly up to the free buffet and shove food into their faces at eleven thirty in the morning. They're comatose by one in the afternoon."

"Excuse me," I said. "You keep referring to a contest. What if I'm just doing everyday handicapping?"

"There's no such thing," said Lackey. "Every bet is a contest bet. Or should be treated as such. And stop interrupting me. The sound of your voice gives me hives.

"A good contest handicapper has an excellent chance to turn a minimal investment into a windfall. I can win at any track on a daily basis but you never will. You will only play contests and you will only play contests that offer full return on investment. There are contests that offer more than full return. They offer prizes for best day totals and so forth. These are the best opportunities. Every bet you make must reflect your intuitive genius. There is never an excuse for a lazy bet. Every bet is your personal truth. There is no before or after in a contest situation. You are defined in the moment of the wager. Any doubt or hesitation will cost you dearly and it has nothing to do with your handicapping ability. It has to do with desire. It's what the child within still craves: attention, love, caring, money, toys, joy.

The night before a contest I review all races at the contest tracks. I note the race conditions, trainers, jocks. If it's a win-only contest any race is playable; field size does not matter. If win and place, six horses is the minimum. Let's say you eliminate a race because of field size and a horse in such a race jumps up and pays $80. You hear the screams and shouts of the players fortunate enough to have the horse. You look at the race and realize it could have been a play. How do you feel?"

"Miserable?" I said.

"Wrong answer, grasshopper," said Lackey. "It never happened! Only your winning bets are real. All else is an imaginary world of fear driven demons waiting to destroy you. You avoid this destruction by creation.

It is between you and the Racing Form. You asked why all wagers should be considered as contest wagers. How could they not? If you *EVER* make a wager borne of speculation or hope or prayer or, God forbid, the need to make money, you diminish your ability to create the future. Every fear-driven act reduces your capacity for wisdom, bravery and wise choices. It's time for you to stop being a putz. It's time for you to recognize that anything is possible!"

CHAPTER FIFTY - FIVE

For the next couple of weeks Lackey had me handicapping four hours a night in preparation for a mock contest the following day. Following his orders I attempted to select the likely favorite in each race. When I went beyond and tried to find the winner I became frustrated. Lackey told me this was the need to gamble asserting itself. As Lackey said, the best way to determine the favorite was by seeing the race through the eyes of the average handicapper, the person influenced by the obvious.

After a minimal breakfast of a plain roll or muffin and a cup of coffee, I sat at the desk playing a make-believe contest in real time. I could play any track I chose. I had twelve win bets to make per day. Lackey sat next to me, observing.

Maybe I was self conscious. Maybe I was out of practice. I selected loser after loser. The more losing bets I recorded the worse I felt.

"I don't think I can do this," I said after a dismal day.

"I thought this was what you wanted."

"I want to. I don't have the ability."

"It has nothing to do with ability. I thought you'd know that by now. For a smart boy you can be pretty stupid. You have oodles of ability. We know that. You're being victimized by unresolved childhood issues. The need to be perfect. The feeling you aren't enough. The sense of being a little boy in a man's world. The craving for approval. Freud would have loved you. He would have written a book about you. He would have called it The Psychology of A Moron."

"What do I do about it?" I said.

"Most of the horses you select are speed horses that tire. Self-doubt drains you of energy. When in such a state your handicapping defaults to facile speed analysis. You see the "1's" in the past performances and you don't have the energy to interpret them correctly. Your lack of energy compels you to select a horse with a similar lack of energy. You are creating, all right, but losers, not winners. Stop micro-handicapping. Don't examine the data so closely. Stop trying! Float above the information. See the big picture. Determine trainer motivation concurrent with evaluation of horse ability. This is about the horse's story, not yours. Taking a walk in the desert when your head is messed up is a good idea. Talk to a cactus. Listen to what it says. It knows more than you do. This is an easy game. Stop making it difficult. Have fun!"

I had no idea how Lackey could have confidence it me. Except for his moans, sighs, or eye-rolling over some of my selections he was constantly supportive.

CHAPTER FIFTY - SIX

I continued handicapping at night and playing mock contests during the day. I couldn't find a rhythm. I rarely put two or three winners together.

One day I had a big-priced horse disqualified. I found myself on tilt, staring into space.

"Lost your concentration?" said Lackey.

"I was thinking about my wife."

"Why?"

"Sometimes I feel the need to talk to someone."

"You mean like a friend?"

"Exactly!" I was gratified Lackey knew what I meant.

"That's your soul saying goodbye to the last vestiges of your humanity. If you want to handicap at the highest level your devotion must be complete."

"You mean I can't have a friend?"

"Sure. Put down the form and go make a friend. Make lots of friends. Get into politics. Join a club. Go back to your AA and GA meetings. Only give up handicapping."

"You make it so black and white."

"Let me ask you," said Lackey. "In your life what's the one thing that has always called to you?"

I thought of the early days with Debra. The thrill of holding hands, the first kiss. The night I proposed. The certainty that love was the true path.

"Handicapping," I said.

"Exactly," said Lackey. "You might have waited until dinner to reveal your sensitive side."

I looked down at The Form. I heard a click and the TVs went to black.

"That's all for today," said Lackey. "You want too much. It's what's standing between you and the appreciation of the data. There's no love in this world. No sublime experience of loving a woman or bringing a child into existence. When are you going to get it?"

"I get it. Please let me continue the contest."

Lackey regarded me impassively. He reached over and turned on the TVs and went through the bamboo curtains. I picked up The Form. I felt like a traitor held in the grip of demon feelings planted by an alcoholic father and uncaring mother. I took a deep breath. It was nine minutes before the 6th at Hawthorne. Plenty of time. $5,000 claimers going a mile and one sixteenth. Eleven runners. I was floating above the data. I took a look at the horse I thought would be the favorite. He had staggered in second in his last two races. He was wildly over bet at 4-5. The fans thought he was the only horse that could walk. Maybe. Maybe not. I absorbed the running lines of all eleven runners in a matter of minutes. The secret was there. The key. I knew I would find it. I wasn't trying to do anything. It felt good.

CHAPTER FIFTY - SEVEN

My handicapping was improving. Lackey had me betting real money. Not much, $20 win bets. Lackey never discussed it but I knew I was turning a profit.

One morning I took a walk in the desert. When I returned to the trailer I stood outside shaking the sand out of my shoes. The door was ajar. I heard Lackey talking to somebody.

"No...I don't think so...right...no way...no...don't press me ...yeah... I know..."

I opened the door. Lackey was sitting on the couch. The second he saw me he took the cell phone from his ear and flipped it shut.

"First race at Calder is in a half hour," he said.

I played well. I was on fire. I became fascinated with my talent. The second that happened I lost concentration. I had a couple of horses run out. The races stopped making sense. I was trying too hard, over-thinking, micro-handicapping. I was staring at a twelve horse field at Fairgrounds. $7,500 claimers which hadn't won three races at a mile. It was like reading Sanskrit. I kept looking back and forth at the screen, noting odds changes, then back at The Form getting more desperate by the second.

"What's going on?" said Lackey.

"It's a tough race," I said.

"You've been looking at that race for fourteen minutes. While you've been grinding your molars into dust a $15,000 maiden paid $41 at Hawthorne and the longest price in a five horse field won the first race at Hollywood."

"There's an angle here. I'm going to find it."

"Put down The Form and listen up." I complied.

Lackey said, "You were probably aware that a little while ago you picked four winners in a row including two cap horses. It froze you, didn't it."

"Yes."

"At the root is the feeling that you don't deserve success, that you're not good enough, one mistake will kill you, you're funny looking, that who-the-hell knows."

I nodded.

"You know better than to try to find the angle in a race. When you're supposed to see the angle you will. Why do you suppose countless decent players see the key to the race right after the race, an angle so obvious they can't believe they missed it?"

"They were looking too hard?"

"Exactly. Need won't get you nothing but a candy apple and a toothache. Okay, back to work."

I glanced back at the Fairgrounds race. Four minutes until post time. I knew better than to impose my perception of the race onto the data. Yet I found myself doing it, looking for the recent claim or barn change or stretch out. I took a deep breath, looked up at the screens, and saw there were nine minutes until the ninth at Aqueduct. $15,000 claimers, non winners of two races. The entirety of equine ability and trainer motivation is evident in such races. I took a look at the rail horse. A bad looking nag. The two horse wasn't much better. The 3 horse was in a new, decent barn and had flashed speed in tougher races in the spring.

I let the data come to me.

CHAPTER FIFTY - EIGHT

I woke in the middle of the night to the sound of an argument. The voices were coming from Lackey's bedroom.

"You fucking bitch, I'll cut your throat."

It was Lackey's voice. I ran in thinking he was in trouble. He was lying on the floor, an oxygen tank at his side, clear tubes running from the top into his nostrils.

"You cunt, you'll never get away with this." His voice was coarse and ragged.

"You can't love me 'cause I play the horses? You think I'm no good? I'll show you, bastards. I'm not a dog. You can't whip me like a dog. I'm a big boy, I don't even shit in my dog pants, I'm a big freaking hero I pet my rooster two times every waking hour you bitch, you sternum vagrant piece of pussy."

I ran into the bathroom, wet a towel, came out and gently lifted him into a sitting position. I held the towel to his forehead and held him.

"Oh, God," he said, "this is a horrible situation, the blasphemy of an uneaten creampuff. I am the killer, why, I have killed my child! How did this happen? Jesus, I blew it!"

After a while Lackey stopped talking. He started crying, high pitched whimpers. I held him until he fell asleep. I picked him up and put him on the bed.

I went back to the couch. I thought about something I rarely permitted myself to consider: why had Lackey taken me into his life? Why me? How had Mitra known about him? How was it that I had gotten those Surf postcards in the first place? Mitra and Lackey: how and why? Glimpsing Lackey's vulnerability had jarred me. Looking at the Racing Form didn't seem so important.

The thing was, there was nothing else.

CHAPTER FIFTY - NINE

Lackey remained in his room the following day. I played a contest. For a guy who six hours before thought handicapping unimportant, I crushed. I was vaguely aware that I was racking up winner after winner. Points, money, were irrelevant. I watched the races as impassively as if I was reading a book. When the last race at Golden Gate went off and I had a 33-1 shot nosed on the wire, I checked my results. My one day total would have won most two day contests.

I suddenly remembered Lackey. I rushed into his room. He was sitting on the side of the bed, dressed for dinner.

"I'm in the mood for fish and chips," he said.

At dinner I told him about my day. About my newfound confidence. About the lack of trying, desire, need or anything else that separated me from the data.

"It was inevitable," he said. As usual he was putting away the beer at a good clip. For a guy who was at death's door a few hours ago he had made a nice recovery.

"The key is to let what happened today become who you are. That takes time and that's something we don't have."

"I have time," I said.

"No you don't," said Lackey. "The World Series Of Handicapping is next week."

"The World Series?"

"Yeah. You're going to be in it."

"It's a $1,000 buy-in," I mumbled. "$1,000." I still had the $500 Mitra had given me. Where was I going to to come up with the other $500?"

"I've already paid it," said Lackey. "Got your hotel room lined up, too."

The thought of playing in one of horseracing's biggest contests was overwhelming. It was a quantum leap from making $20 bets in a Victorville trailer to competing against six hundred of the best handicappers in the world.

"I assume you're going," I said.

"No, my young hero, you're going to fly solo. There's nothing else I can teach you. You know the game. It has nothing to do with numbers. You know what it takes to create the winner.

What you will come up against at The Orleans is yourself. We haven't had a chance to destroy the demons who are ready to feast on your fear, frustration and indecision. That's okay. Rely on your intuitive knowledge to bring you to the precipice of the wager. And then...and then..." he took a swig of beer and belched.

"And then what?" I said.

"Take the leap of faith. Never be afraid. You are all you need."

CHAPTER SIXTY

A couple of days before I was to leave we went to Target. Lackey bought me some new shirts and jeans. He thought it was important to look good.

"I don't know why," he said. "It's not like clothes make the man. But they don't hurt."

We spent our last day hanging out, eating, and discussing the contest.

"Registration is next Wednesday at nine am. You'll get to the hotel on Tuesday afternoon. Maybe watch a basketball game. Have a nice dinner. The hotel has a good Chinese restaurant. The steak house is overpriced, the service is slow, and not much better than the buffet. If you like clam chowder the clam bar has a decent Manhattan. Maybe take in a movie.

On Wednesday get down to the registration area no later than eight am. When the doors open at nine go straight to the seat you want and reserve it. The shock at not playing in a Victorville trailer will be significant. Don't worry about it. Get the day's forms and handicap in real time. No bets. Get familiar with your seat. At about five o'clock get the contest racing forms, grab a nice dinner, go upstairs and do your night before handicapping. Lights out at 11 o'clock."

"What if I can't sleep? I've had insomnia in previous

contests."

"Do your little serenity prayer. Or try Public Television. It'll put you right out."

"Play loose," continued Lackey. "If you feel cold or tight or incapable of making a bet make one or two anyway. Get the juices flowing. Have fun. It's all a cosmic joke, anyway. You'll pick up a rhythm. You'll be fine."

He spoke not a word about what kind of races to bet. In any case, most of my time with Lackey had less to do with handicapping and more with putting myself in a position to access my intuition.

CHAPTER SIXTY - ONE

On the day I left Lackey wasn't around. When I got into my little Neon, on the seat I found a receipt for additional month's rent for the car and $1,000 in cash. The Neon started right up. I went down D Street and picked up the 15 North.

I pulled into the Orleans self- parking lot just after four in the afternoon. I checked in and they treated me like royalty. Lackey had reserved a suite in the new tower.

The suite was large enough for a family of four. Besides the bed there were a couple of couches, a full kitchen, two huge plasma TVs, a wet bar and a bathroom with a small Jacuzzi. At about six I went down and had a noodle dish in the Chinese restaurant and, as Lackey had promised, it was great. I went for a long walk after dinner down Las Vegas Boulevard. It didn't take long before the glitz and glamour of The Strip gave way to shoddy apartments that had signs like $60 MOVES YOU IN stapled to railings.

Back in the room I soaked in the Jacuzzi and got into bed and watched a few minutes of Law And Order. I called down and left two wakeup calls, one for 6:30 and one for 7. I read a couple of pages from the bedside Bible before falling into a deep sleep.

I must have been tired because I slept straight through. I shaved, showered, and went downstairs, got a coffee and a copy of the LA Times and took an escalator up to the Mardi Gras Ballroom, site of the World Series. There were already about twenty players in line. They seemed to know one another. Nervous energy roiled in my stomach. I hadn't felt it for a while. I closed my eyes. The whole venture seemed idiotic. The only thing I felt capable of creating was my own destruction

CHAPTER SIXTY - TWO

When the doors opened I got a seat at a corner table with decent sightlines to eight TVs. The TVs weren't in front of me like at Lackey's but at an angle. It would take some getting used to. I picked up the day's Racing Forms. I was tempted to get the next day's contest papers but I wanted to follow Lackey's advice.

I had trouble concentrating. Without Lackey looking over my shoulder or the imperative of a contest, I didn't have focus. Also, every few minutes a fellow player would take a seat at my table and introduce himself. There were nine chairs at my round table. By three o'clock they were all taken.

I made no bets but got a sense of how the tracks were playing. Aqueduct was wet, so was Calder, but Hawthorne and the west coast tracks were dry. If they would remain that way was anyone's guess.

At four o'clock I scooped up the contest forms and went up to the room. I read the Bible and then went down and had tofu in oyster sauce with string beans at the excellent Chinese restaurant. I bought a Macanudo Portofino cigar at a place call Terrible's and smoked as I took a stroll up Las Vegas Boulevard. The night was clear and warm and the cigar was delicious.

I got up to the room at about 6:30. I spent the next four hours handicapping. I was able to assign favoritism in most races. It was the races where I couldn't that interested me the most. It meant they were wide open. I circled eight or nine of those races, took a shower, and crawled into bed. I left two wakeups, one for 6:30 and one for 7:00 am.

Every fifteen minutes or so I turned the lights on and watched TV. I flicked from Leno to Letterman to the Weather channel to CNN, looking for the perfect entertainment or news story. I began to get nervous. What if I couldn't go to sleep?

I turned off the light. I thought of a time when I was a kid, playing in the most beautiful park with my best friend, Andy. A small brook gurgled behind pink flowers. The next thing I knew the phone was ringing with my 6:30 am wakeup call.

CHAPTER SIXTY - THREE

Just after eight I took the escalator up to the ballroom. When I walked through the door I felt the energy. It was like entering a house of worship, although this was a place where very few believers would have their prayers answered.

I took my seat and organized my Racing Forms into a booklet and then got the scratches. It was two hours before the first contest race. Everybody in the room felt like they had a chance to win.

I flipped through The Forms. I was too nervous to study. I got up and walked around, watched hundreds of old, overweight, mostly white guys staring at racing papers, computers, and scratch sheets. I wondered how many of them had tied their self worth to the process. Was that what I had done? What if I conveyed this thought to Lackey? I could hear him laughing and saying, "Well now, what self would that be?"

I was taking myself too seriously. It had to be about having fun. That was the only way to open the channel to the intuitive sense. I sat back down. My heart was pounding. Several of my tablemates greeted me. One of them asked which tracks I'd be playing. I had no idea. There were five tracks from which to make our bets: Calder in Florida; Aqueduct in New York; Hawthorne in Chicago; and Hollywood Park and Golden Gate out west. I thought back to the last time I was at Hollywood Park, digging up the backstretch with a garden tool. To see if I could find the spot where my brother and a horse had disappeared. I had left my wife to do that. What colossal gifts of love and compassion I had squandered on my way to this seat in The Orleans Hotel and Casino.

I glanced at the Racing Forms. I mechanically filled out the contest cards with my name and contest number. Twelve bets a day, win and place format, thirty six bets over three days that would define my place in the Universe.

I got up and took the escalator downstairs. I walked through the casino where the dissolute were staring at price lines, swigging booze, and living and dying at games of chance. I was riveted by the light at the front entrance. The door opened mechanically as I approached and I walked outside into the brilliant daylight, among the hopeful and valets and concierges.

I looked out at the parking lot and beyond, to the distant haze of the mountains and to the bright canopy of blue sky over Las Vegas and the freedom which had always called and which I had ignored.

A woman walked past and I watched her wheel a small suitcase to the entrance. She was beautiful. I gazed at the bright-light freedom one last time, wheeled, and went back into the hotel.

CHAPTER SIXTY - FOUR

That first day I went nothing for twelve on my bets. In the middle of the fiasco I ate a big corned beef sandwich and two pieces of pie. You'd think just by luck I would have hit a bet. I had lost the gift.

When I got back up to the room my brother was sitting on the edge of the desk. Dressed in his silks. It had been a while.

"Did you miss me?" he asked.

"Sure," I said. I had always loved my brother. I mean, I had to. My parents didn't love him, or me. It was them against us. At the time I didn't realize it. I thought it was three against one. Later I saw the deal. We both wanted to be taken care of. That was the problem. You can't be an adult and need to be taken care of. At some point you grow up and take care of yourself. Or don't and become a pathetic piece of shit.

My brother began to de-materialize. In seconds he was gone.

I thought about going downstairs. Getting the next day's Racing Forms and establishing the morning lines. Why? I had no shot.

I laid on the bed and tried watching TV. No dice. I went down to the casino and tried a couple of hands of blackjack. Busted in six consecutive hands. For lack of anything better to do I wandered over to the Race and Sports book and picked up the next day's Racing Forms. The second they were under my arm I calmed down.

I somehow fell asleep. When I awoke sun was streaming through the window. I checked the clock. Seven. I hadn't set a wakeup call. I guess part of me was resigned to getting in my car and leaving Vegas. Instead I showered, shaved, got dressed, grabbed the Forms and went downstairs. Over a Seattle's Best I looked through the papers. Nothing made sense. Fuck it, I thought. I'll finish up the contest. Let's see if it's possible to pick thirty-six consecutive losers.

CHAPTER SIXTY - FIVE

Maybe my surrender opened the channel to my intuition. I made my first bet in the third at Aqueduct. It was a sprint and a cheap little speed horse had been claimed by a nobody and jumped up three levels to a tough spot. But the track had been playing fast, there was no other speed, and the apprentice was live. My horse won by open lengths and paid $26.

I felt no big joy. It was okay to handicap horses. Lackey's words about permission resonated.

I glanced at the next race at Calder. Pathetic maidens. Why, here was a horse that was stretching out, had been mired on the wood in his last two races, made good speed and lost by about a hundred lengths in his previous effort. Sometimes that's better than one. Solid trainer, live rider, no other discernible speed, all systems go. He was 42-1 and I took the leap of faith. He won by open lengths and paid $87.

I didn't scream or celebrate. Not even after a $22 winner in an Aqueduct maiden special, or a little wire to wire $50 bomb from the 12 hole at Hawthorne, or the blinkers off first timer on the Hollywood turf who wired a dull field of one other than's at 8-1. There was an Irish bred horse in a turf sprint at Hollywood Park making his second start in the country after a horrible first out on the dirt. He didn't have much to beat. He aired and paid $16. I checked the betting receipts in my back pocket to make sure I wasn't dreaming. A sense of calm persisted.

When the day was over I had hit seven of twelve winners. My lowest price horse paid $12. When I checked the leader board I was startled to see my name on top.

I went up to my room and sat on the edge of the bed. I was a horse race handicapper. I had what it takes. I had the ability to be in the moment, the freedom to follow intuition unfettered by fear.

I thought of Debra, my honey, wife, my soul-mate. I fished the cell phone out of my pocket. It had been a long time since Debra and I talked. Back then I was equivocating about my reasons for coming to California. That didn't matter. I was a success. I was on the threshold of greatness.

I punched in her numbers. She answered on the third ring.

"Hi, honey," I said. Silence.

"Deb?" I said. "It's me. Sid."

"I know who it is," she said.

"Deb, baby... I know this is a bit weird to be calling you. But I wanted to share what's happening here with somebody…ah…with you. I wanted to tell you about the strangest thing."

"What is it, Sid. What?"

"I'm in Las Vegas in a big horserace handicapping contest. And it all kind of came together, I'm in first place and there's a huge prize pool and I'm going to win the damn thing, can you believe it? And honey, with the money I'm going to make I'm thinking we can buy a house and we can make a baby and hell, I can't believe this is happening and I wanted to share it with you."

"You're in Vegas. Playing the horses. That's what you're telling me."

"Well yeah, but I'm winning, honey, I'm not a loser. I'm not a deadbeat screenwriter. I'm a great handicapper. I think I always was but I just couldn't accept it."

I held the phone against my ear into the silence.

"I'm glad you're happy, Sid. But when you left to play the horses—"

"No, Debra, to find my brother--:"

"---to play the horses and you broke my heart. I don't want to see you. I can't... I've... I've filed for divorce. Let me know an address if and when you have one and my attorney will get you the papers."

"Divorce? Papers? What are you talking about?"

"Don't you get it, Sid? Don't you remember what our relationship was based on? Love, not money. Trust, not broken promises. You don't have room in your life for horses and another person. You know that. It's an obsession, it never ends. That's why you got sober and became abstinent. Don't act surprised. I'm glad you're winning the contest. Why don't you take some of that money and buy a whore or, better yet, get yourself a shrink."

She didn't sound angry. She was real calm.

"Debra, please, it's over, this is my last contest. And I did come out here to find my brother and this all just came about. I had a mentor in Victorville and he showed me how I could transcend my fear and... Please, I'm begging you."

"Sid. It's over. You're no use to me. Don't call me again. And I pity the woman who accepts you for what you are, for she'll be getting a shell of a man and a bum deal."

I felt a weary resignation.

"I'm sorry, Deb. I thought you'd be happy."

"You're nuts, Sid."

"Please, Deb."

"Take care of yourself. Let me know when my attorney can send you the papers." The phone went dead.

I sat on the bed for a while. I cried large tears of self pity. After a while I calmed down. I went over to the mini bar and downed three or four small bottles of booze without looking at the labels. The alcohol warmed me... and then it turned.

I looked at the TV, the fucking TV. I grabbed it, yanked it out of the wall and heaved it across the room against the huge plate glass window. There was a blast and smoke as TV tubes shattered but the window didn't break. I grabbed a chair and smashed it into the window over and over. It was like the window was made of titanium. I heard sirens and alarms and the next thing I knew I was yelling and

174

swearing and a guy who must have weighed three hundred pounds and smelled like tuna fish was sitting on my stomach.

CHAPTER SIXTY - SIX

When I got out of jail I stood on the sidewalk blinking at the sun. I rubbed my face. Stubble. I must have been in for a few days. There wasn't much around except for a couple of bail bondsman offices, a hair salon, and a bunch of cinderblock warehouses.

I began walking. I had a vague recollection of coming to California to find my brother. Beyond that everything was a blur. I kept walking. The sun was almost directly overhead. It had to be about noon. I reached into my right pants pocket and discovered a fistful of bills. At least I could eat. But I wasn't hungry.

While I waited at a traffic light a small bird, maybe it was a sparrow, hopped about on a nearby sidewalk. Its head swiveled around in jerky movements. A water bug dangled from its beak. The sidewalk was crystalline. Pieces of shiny glass were embedded in the concrete. Cars whipped by in the background. The water bug's legs were wriggling. I could almost hear it cry for help. "Sidney," it was saying in a female voice. "Whatever are you doing, Sidney?"

I was about to answer when I was aware of a large black car idling beside me. I looked up and saw a brown-skinned woman with a huge nose staring at me through the open window.

"Sidney," she repeated, "has the sun fried what's left of your New York brain? Do you not remember your gin buddy from The Surf motel in Los Angeles?"

My gin partner. I studied her brown eyes. Wide grinning mouth. There were other people in the car. I looked down. The bird on the sidewalk fixed me with a withering stare and flew off with the squirming bug.

Of course. Mitra. Mitra Singh. From The Surf Motel. Mitra of Yoo Hoo and cable movies and gin and angry husband and See's lollipops and beer and handicapping and love and death---

"Hello, Mitra," I said.

"Ah, Sidney," she said, emerging from the car. "Why don't you climb aboard. We are staying at a discount hotel over on Paradise Road. What a name for a street in this land of waste and desperation. But so it is, so it shall be."

She held the door open. I could discern a hulking form in the back seat behind the driver. A scream of horror and loss echoed from the car and across the bow of my soul. I could smell doom and resolve pulsing from the stinking, whining idle of the engine.

"I think I'll walk, Mitra," I said.

"Ah, Sidney," she said. "Always failing to take the easy way." She leaned into the car.

CHAPTER SIXTY - SEVEN

I recognized Lemmons, the trainer of Princess Bride, the second he emerged from the back seat. In his hand was an ugly leather sap which he slapped eagerly against his hip.

"Hi, Sid," he said. I looked from Mitra to Lemmons again and again. How did they know one another?

"I have nothing to say to you. What's this about?"

"You're a stupid little fuck, you know that?" said Lemmons. "You had a chance to make big money and you acted like a fool."

"Please, Mr. Lemmons, please watch the tone, Sid is a good man, wayward, yes, but good," said Mitra. "Come with us Sidney. It will do no harm to talk with us."

"About what, Mitra? What am I going to talk to you about?"

I watched as another man got out of the back seat. Much slower and more gingerly than Lemmons. It was Lackey.

"My God, it's not easy to get out of the back seat of a car," he said.

"Mr. Lackey," I said. "What's going on? I don't understand."

"Haven't you learned anything, grasshopper?" said Lackey. "To quote the venerable Werner Erhard, understanding's the booby prize."

I dug my thumbnails into my index fingers to make certain I could feel and this whole scene wasn't a hallucination. It hurt.

"Come on, Sid," continued Lackey, "and we'll try to make sense of what you did in that Orleans Hotel room. You know, going crazy and getting tossed out of the contest and forfeiting all that dough. We'll talk about it and have macaroni and cheese and try to resurrect the Sid I knew in Victorville, a great handicapper and soul most immortal."

Victorville. I felt sick thinking about it. The contest. Debra. What I had won and sacrificed.

"Well, Mr. Lackey and Mitra and Bob, with all due respect, why don't you all go fuck yourselves. I have no idea what you're doing together or if you're figment of my imagination but I've gotta walk and just walk and walk until I sweat enough to somehow purify what's left of my sorry ass."

"Sidney, you are a fine man with your whole life in front of you," said Mitra. "There's nothing so terrible that cannot be undone. In any event, do not be so dramatic. After all, you have not murdered someone, Sidney."

"That's what you think," I said.

There was nothing more to say. I turned and started to walk. I heard footsteps behind me and before I could turn the sap smashed into the side of my head and there was thunderous pain and blackness so profound it transcended the deepest sleep.

CHAPTER SIXTY - EIGHT

When I woke I was lying on a hotel bed. Mitra was sitting next to me, holding a glass of water against my lips. Sitting in chairs across from me were Lackey and Lemmons.

"Ah," said Mitra, "the golden boy has come back to the world of the living."

"Golden boy my ass," said Lemmons. "The little cocksucker had $400,000 in his grubby little hands and blew it."

"I had what?" I said.

"Sid, you were doing it, my boy, you had accessed the genius," said Mitra. "You were in first place in that horserace game and on your way to the heavenly victory. But you lost your way, dear boy, and I know why but it doesn't matter. Because all that counts is that you get back on the horse, that's a funny one, and we'll get you up and running and playing and winning and fulfilling your destiny."

"Of course," said Lemmons, "Mr. Lackey has his own petty motive for wanting you back in action."

"Does needing a new heart constitute a petty motivation?" said Lackey. "I don't think so, you washed up has-been."

"Please," said Mitra, "may we please have couth in this room? Harsh words will accomplish nothing."

Everybody quieted down. Mitra said to me, "Would you like

some soup? I also have the Nabisco cheese and crackers from the vending machine. Salty but delicious."

"No thanks," I said. I felt a pang of affection for her.

"And I think you deserve an answer as to how this has come to pass," said Mitra. "Listen now. Long ago and far away your brother came to this coast and began his career as a race rider. And yet all he ever talked about was you, Sidney. How he looked up to you, your spirit, your soul, your ability to handicap the horse races. I learned all this from my sister Bernice, the owner of Princess Bride."

"Bernice Singh," I whispered.

"And so he rode," continued Mitra, "and it was as if he rode not to win for the owners or trainers but for you, for some misbegotten love or acceptance that you and he never received. No one knows what happened to John. I believe it was a pressure that built within him until finally it burst and he exploded into the desire of his small being."

"And took my goddamn horse with him," said Lemmons.

"I knew when John disappeared he would never return," said Mitra. "There are some things that are known to men and others that remain conjecture…but that John would never be found was understood. An entity would have to replace him. I knew that would always be so. And so you appeared at The Surf one fine November day."

"I was here to find my brother," I said.

"No," said Mitra, "you were here to descend into the darkness of a loveless hell from which you were spawned."

"Easy, Mitra," said Lackey.

"There is no other way to put it, Mr. Lackey. Sidney, your brother's disappearance created the reason for your coming to us, to ride to his rescue, so to speak. You replaced him in body and spirit. Instead of riding a horse you would be riding a racing paper. Not so poetic, true, but completing the great mandala nevertheless."

"And you had to fuck it up. Over a broad," said Lemmons. I winced every time he smacked the sap against his thigh.

"And you sent me The Surf postcards?" I asked Mitra.

"Yes. I sent you the postcards and you came and it could not have been otherwise, for it was destiny, was it not? And so when you appeared I contacted Mr. Lemmons and when it became apparent you were ready to embrace your descent we collaborated to, how do you say, whet your desire. Then Mr. Lackey stepped in to facilitate the process."

"And all this was about winning a horserace contest?"

"Not simply a contest. Contests! Once you could accept your inability to be human the horizon was infinite. You would become a handicapping machine, going from contest to contest decimating the competition, a robo-handicapper, Sidney, a champion, that is the man you would become."

"It's my fault," said Lackey, "I knew you weren't ready. I never should have entered you at The Orleans. It was too soon with Debra and all. You needed more time. But, hell, I need a heart and I was selfish."

"And so I was being used by all of you."

"To fulfill your destiny, Sidney!" said Mitra. "Do not blame us for that. We were helping, don't you see? You could no sooner be human and live a happy life with your little Debbie-girl than I could fly a space ship. You were born and raised to feel or to believe in nothing and that is all you needed to become the greatest handicapper of all time."

I sighed. "Now what?"

"Well, you fucked up, boy," said Lemmons. "By getting thrown out of the Orleans you forfeited the Orleans prize money. But that's okay. Lackey'll take you back down to Victorville and work with you and whip you into proper shape and you'll go back and do the right thing."

"Hey," said Lackey, we had a good time in the desert, didn't we?"

"Yeah," I said.

I was real still for a couple of moments. Then I sat up and punched Mitra in the face. The bones in her nose made a cracking sound. I leaped off the bed and drove a couple of hard rights into where I thought Lackey's heart would be, if he had one. I saw him whipsaw backward a second before I saw Lemmons swinging the sap and my head exploded.

CHAPTER SIXTY - NINE

As I lay on the bed in some motel room, every bone in my body hurt. Blood seeped out of wounds onto the bedspread. I was thirsty but each time I tried to get up my muscles froze. I was hoping I wasn't dead.

I never saw the double-cross coming. I wasn't certain I would have done it any other way. If it was my life I had to give so be it. I put it on the line after a lifetime of flight and it was worth it.

I didn't miss the money. The jubilation I felt after doing well in the contest had nothing to do with money. It was about my love for Debra. My dream of being a great handicapper was about love the whole time.

I missed Debra but I knew there was no going back. She was a beautiful soul but not my soul mate. The only soul mate was that shrimp of a younger brother who saw within me what I could not see within myself. The brother who huddled in the foxholes with me as the war between our mother and father raged. My little brother who had summoned me and put me on the path.

I coughed and blood cascaded from my mouth. I wondered if Lemmons and Mitra knew I was alive. Maybe the beating wasn't supposed to kill me, just punish me.

That they had manipulated me mattered not at all. That they might be responsible for my death was irrelevant. They had liberated me. I was finished trying to convince another human being of anything. As I pondered my newfound freedom I heard a restless demon whisper, "Sidney. Who are you kidding, you huge loser. I'm hungry. Let's have some pie."

I smiled and embraced this voice, this voice which tried to kill me and always would. My only problem had been trying to deny it. It was like denying it was my legs that let me walk or eyes which gave me sight. The voice of my loathing gave boundaries to my joyous self, as death does to life, and if the demon voice did not exist I would have no earthly substance.

The thought occurred to call 911 but I didn't have the energy. It felt like the end. I thought of a nameless, faceless woman, someone who might have mothered my child, and sadness briefly filled me. She was out there, waiting, and would for a tiny eternity.

I heard a rustling sound outside. Perhaps Lemmons had come back to finish me. He wouldn't take me lying down. I staggered to my feet and took slow, tiny steps to the door, palms pressed against the wall, leaving bloody prints in their wake.

I finally got to the door, pulled off the chain, and yanked it open. Several feet beyond the asphalt apron of the parking lot was my brother, clad in his cerise jockey silks, astride Princess Bride. The pink saddlecloth with the number 8 flapped against her powerful sides. She pawed the hard surface with a massive hoof, nostrils flaring, ears pricked. My brother was wearing a huge grin, his body almost translucent in the shimmering dusk, radiating acceptance and love.

John's sinewy body was framed by the desert sky. Behind him cars whizzed by on Paradise Road, blazing fireflies trailing in their wake. Beyond the lights of Las Vegas was a range of mountains I had never seen, and above a twinkling night sky of vision and hope.

My brother reached out his arm. My wounds had ceased to bleed or hurt. I extended my hand, he grasped me, and in a powerful motion swung me into the saddle behind him.

Princess Bride loped to a canter, then a full out gallop, racing across the pavement as a gentle wind played on my face like a lover's touch.

All I had known, wanted, craved, or believed, receded and vanished into the embrace of another lifetime.

Made in the USA
Las Vegas, NV
11 May 2022

48745932R00105